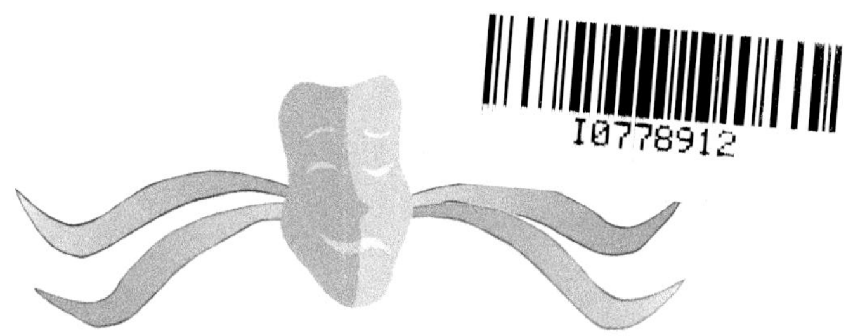

Neither of them noticed the package of trouble hurtling towards them until Amanita was extracting herself from under a jumble of girl, longbow, and brilliantly colored arrows that seemed to have spilled everywhere.

"Ooops," said the new girl without a great deal of regret. She looked up at them with a certain wide-eyed innocence that Thony couldn't help but feel was a bit of a put-on.. Her leather jerkin was criss-crossed by a shoulder sheathe for a rather long sword, considering her size, that she was trying to untangle from her longbow and quiver.

"Don't you believe in looking where you're going?" Amanita demanded irritably.

"Usually," the girl replied. "Sometimes. Um... occasionally?"

The greasy-seeming horse-dealer from earlier in the morning was also bearing down on them, his face furious.

Amanita's gaze narrowed as she looked between the new girl and the new arrivals.

"What's the matter here?" she demanded. "That girl just released all me stock," the greasy guy snarled. "She's goin' t'pay for this trouble!"

Amanita looked over her shoulder. "Did you really do that?"

The girl shuffled her feet and looked down – to hide a self-satisfied smirk, Thony rather thought.

"Eh... heh-heh-heh-heh-heh," she chuckled uncomfortably, but didn't deny it.

So You Want to Be a Hero?

Book Three of the Prankster Prince

Mangala McNamara

Rising Dragon Books

Also available in eBook and hardcover editions.
McNamara, Kerridwen Mangala
So You Want to Be a Hero?/ by Mangala McNamara Indiana: Rising Dragon Books, 2024
 p. 178, 1 map
(McNamara, Mangala. The Prankster Prince; bk. 3)
Summary: Prince Thony's adventure to find a princess-bride is derailed when he and his friend, Amanita, get stuck in a small town that is on the verge of being overwhelmed by an Evil Wizard and his army.ISBN 978-1-960160-30-0 (pbk)
1. Princes and princesses - Fiction. 2. Adolescent Rebellion - Fiction
ISBN 978-1-960160-31-7 (hc) ISBN 978-1-960160-28-7 (eBook)

ISBN: 978-1-960160-30-0
First Print Edition: March 2024
10 9 8 7 6 5 4 3 2 1

For everyone who finds themselves in a situation too big
for them to handle – and who decides to keep on and
find a 'sideways solution.'

And for my kids, whose reaction to this book was
"What do you mean you're not writing the next one for
four months?"

CONTENTS

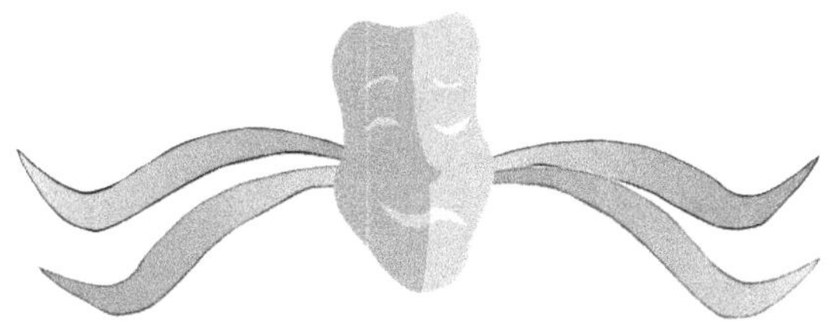

Chapter ONE

Trouble in Small Packages

"WELL, AT LEAST BREAKFAST WASN'T quite as bad as dinner," Thony said as the pair of them exited the Inn of the Starred Hoof. "And the innkeeper *did* give us directions to where there's a guy selling horses."

Amanita *humphed* over this assessment.

"Not that we *need* to buy a packhorse," Thony added with a certain asperity as he followed her into the attached stables.'

"It was an excuse to ask for directions," the fluffy-haired girl said nonchalantly. "And an excuse to wander around town."

Thony rolled his eyes. He knew that. But it might get a little awkward with the innkeeper when they never actually showed up with another horse after she'd haggled over the cost of stabling for a third beast.

Not that they should likely be paying even as much as whatever Puck had paid for this slovenly mess of a place. The young prince wrinkled his nose and squinted his eyes against the heavy reek. The daylight sneaking in the cracks between the wall-boards didn't improve the place over what they, thankfully, *hadn't* seen the night before when they'd brought the equines into this place.

"Sorry, Twinklestar," he said as they came to the stalls holding their four-footed friends.

Not that his and Amanita's room was anything like luxurious, but at least it was clean.

The unicorn eyed him with irritation.

"Actually," Amanita said thoughtfully, "this isn't as bad as I thought it was last night. I mean it *smells* just as bad, but all the muck has been swept into that one corner. And there's fresh hay spread in the stalls – well," she temporized as Twinklestar snorted, "Fresh*er* hay, anyways."

Thony was checking the troughs for feed and water. "The oats are good. And the water is clean. The innkeeper *did* say he hasn't been able to hire help since the Raven troops took over the town. But it also looked like he hadn't had paying customers with horses for awhile – so maybe he just hadn't felt he needed to clean up?"

Amanita gave the disdainful little sniff of someone who had been a professional at this sort of thing. "You shouldn't leave stuff in this state."

Thony shrugged. "Yeah, but if it's just him and his wife and that little boy of theirs – I imagine keeping the innroom ready and having stuff to serve the people who come in for a meal is probably his first priority." He paused. "It was nice of him to get up early to take care of the stables now that he *does* have paying guests using it."

Twinklestar seemed amused, but not inclined to explain.

"That's just his *job*," Amanita said, rather less forgivingly, but then she relented. "But yeah, this is good. I was thinking we either had to clean it all up ourselves or else move Twinkie and Silverfoot somewhere else."

Thony recalled what a meticulous job she had insisted on doing in cleaning the hallway when he had first met her and had visions of Amanita forcing him to scrub the stable floor on his hands and knees, packed earth though it was. On the other hand, Puck had already paid for stabling here and he himself probably shouldn't be squandering what funds he had, since there was no way to replace them once they were gone.

"Let's go 'look' for that packhorse," he suggested before Amanita's neat-nut nature could manifest again. "We'll take you guys out for some exercise later," he promised the equines. Twinklestar let him know that it had been a long journey and he and Silverfoot were entirely prepared to rest peacefully for a couple days – but that a brief turn about the neighborhood to stretch their legs would be appreciated... perhaps after lunch.

An hour or so later, Thony seriously wanted to object to Amanita's characterization of Flowerdust as a 'small town.'

Granted, he'd never been farther than the nearest villages in Aldyrwald, and both of those were literally in the shadow of his father's castle. And neither of those had more than a half-dozen streets. And it took both villages to have all the necessary artisans – they were really more like one really extended village, but the residents insisted they were separate and had separate village councils and inter-village competitions and made a Big Deal if a girl from one village wanted to marry a young man from the other one. *(Although you should have **heard** the caterwauling that had gone on when one of the local milkmaids went off to marry a cheesemaker from one of the neighboring valleys that* *was also part of Aldyrwald's demesne. Her mother had carried on as if the girl was* **dying,** *not moving a few leagues away. Thony was just as glad he hadn't had to hear the parents of one of Queen Janet's maids from Schwannsberg who had fallen for one of Papa's footmen and decided to stay in Aldyrwald.)*

But Flowerdust – for all the disparaging comments that Amanita kept making – had a whole *row* of shops for clothes. Two tailors, a seamstress, an embroiderer, and a fellow who sold hats and gloves and fans and other fripperies that apparently were brought in from elsewhere. Not to mention the shop that just sold bolts of cloth, and the *three* shoemakers and two jewelers.

There were so many streets that the young prince couldn't keep them straight in his head; the streets even had names. *(Amanita said that in* **real** *cities the names of the streets were on sign-posts, like the names of the inns and taverns. Though they were usually done with pictures, not necessarily written in words.)*

Thony had counted at least three taverns – two of them without inns attached. *(Amanita called those 'restaurants' and said people went there only to eat.)* There had been at least two smiths, a saddlery, a *glassmaker,* three shops selling herbs and simples, and a shop that sold nothing but fresh-cut *flowers.*

There was a central open, cobbled square in front of a rather gigantic building that wasn't a castle but wasn't far from it. Farmers from the outlying areas and traders from visiting caravans had gathered there, just like on the market-day in the villages by the Devinthals' castle back home, each with a stall to sell his or her goods... And what goods! Thony had never seen such a profusion of fruits and vegetables and more bolts of cloth and ribbons and...

And there were *people* in all those shops and walking briskly from place to place, ignoring most of the others around them and greeting only the occasional person. Some were dressed in very fine clothes, and others in what was clearly working-wear. Kids, were there, too – again, some quite well-dressed, and others of them quite grubby and with a look to their faces that made Thony feel awkward in a familiar way – like they wanted something from him that he didn't have the ability to give. *(Rather like the citizens of Aldyrwald, but **they** were expecting Thony to grow up and be their king. These kids should have no such expectations...)*

And they hadn't made it halfway through the 'town.'

Thony was practically reeling – and it wasn't from hunger. Amanita had insisted they stop and purchase a snack from one of the farmers and he was pleasantly munching on the last bits of a roll that had sausage baked into it and had actual *flavor,* unlike what he sincerely hoped was the unpalatable-but-nourishing stuff at the Inn of the Starred Hoof.

Amanita, by contrast was fuming.

"That innkeeper," she growled as she stalked through the streets, Thony following her a half-pace behind since he had no idea where they were going now. "I can't believe he sent us – sent *you,* a *unicorn-maiden* – to such a shoddy excuse for a horse-dealer."

Oh, yes, they'd *also* been to the outskirts of town to visit a horse-trader. And she wasn't far wrong about the quality of the beasts they'd seen. Even the poorest farmers in Aldyrwald didn't try to get work out of such swaybacked, toothless, old animals. And the man selling them had seemed kind of... icky. He'd left Thony with a feeling like he wanted to wash his hands after being in the man's vicinity.

And that had been before Thony had gotten close enough to see the galls and lash-marks on some of the horses' hides. He'd felt sick looking at them, but the price the man was quoting them for even the least brokendown equine – a dispirited-looking donkey – had made it clear that rescuing the lot of them was beyond the young prince's abilities. Or at least his purse.

"He *did* say there wasn't much available for sale since the Raven troops came in," Thony pointed out, ignoring the other thrust of the girl's complaint. They'd decided to have him keep wearing the crystal-white unicorn-maiden *robe* in order to maintain their... well, it wasn't really a *disguise,* given that Twinklestar *had* Chosen Thony...

Actually, the innkeeper had implied that there wasn't much of *anything* around for sale, perhaps trying to excuse the poor quality of the food he'd offered them. But everywhere Thony looked, there was absolute profusion...

Amanita snorted. "If I'd crossed his palm with copper, doubtless he'd have 'suddenly remembered' someone with better horses to sell. And if I'd crossed it with *silver...*" She shook her head fiercely.

Thony blinked in surprise. He'd read about this. "You mean *bribe* him?"

Amanita shrugged. "Compensate him for the information, I suppose. Nothing in it for him to tell us for free after all."

The young prince told himself he didn't need to be shocked. It was... apparently just how things were *done* in cities.

Or, um, *towns.*

But... in Aldyrwald and its villages... information was free. Especially information like directions to somewhere or some person.

Amanita had paused on a street-corner and was looking at him with a tilted head.

"Don't tell me the same thing doesn't happen in Aldyrwald," she said. "I got sent down from the castle kitchens to buy eggs and cream and stuff at the market a few times. And I bought them from the 'wrong' vendor because nobody told me who to buy them from and this other girl had better prices."

Thony frowned. "I assume we have some sort of long-running agreement to make sure that the castle is supplied regularly. Though... I'd think that would mean we'd get *better* prices as a regular customer..."

She gave him an almost pitying look. "This was for extra stuff, not the regular deliveries. And I'm pretty sure some of the profit from those higher prices goes straight back into the Chief Cook's pocket. Or maybe *Paul's,*" she mused. "That would be just like him."

Paul had been her nemesis during her brief tenure as an apprentice pastry chef.

Thony wanted to speak up and defend his people... but he hadn't seen what she had... and he wasn't sure how to do so without actual evidence...

...and Amanita was looking at him with that condescending expression...

...so neither of them noticed the package of trouble hurtling towards them until Amanita was extracting herself from under a jumble of girl, longbow, and brilliantly colored arrows that seemed to have spilled everywhere.

"Ooops," said the new girl without a great deal of regret. She looked up at them with a certain wide-eyed innocence that Thony couldn't help but feel was a bit of a put-on. Her hair was pulled back from her face in a partial ponytail, with the rest of it hanging down to just above her shoulders. Her leather jerkin was criss-crossed by a shoulder sheathe for a rather long sword, considering her size, that she was trying to untangle from her longbow and quiver.

"Don't you believe in looking where you're going?" Amanita demanded irritably.

"Usually," the girl replied, absently accepting Thony's hand to stand back up and patting herself all over. "Sometimes. Um... *occasionally?*" She gave Thony a measuring look. "You're stronger than you look."

The young prince hoped he kept his wince internal. Proper Princely Behavior had demanded that he offer assistance – unless he knew he'd likely get socked for it, as with Amanita – and he'd forgotten that he was dressed up as a unicorn-maiden and wasn't supposed to act like a prince – or a *boy* – at all.

"Um, yeah, about that," he began uncomfortably.

The girl shrugged. "No problemo. People always underestimate unicorn-maidens. I should know. One of my best friends is one."

Thony exchanged an alarmed look with Amanita – they'd been counting on no one in the area being familiar enough with unicorns to be able to call their bluff.

Not that it *was* exactly a bluff.

Thony *was* a unicorn-maiden, since Twinklestar had Chosen him and he'd accepted *(after a great deal of resistance, and only after he found out it wasn't a lifelong commitment).*

But he was a *boy,* and unicorn-maidens *weren't.*

And right now, he was dressed up in a white unicorn-maiden *robe* that was the remains of the usual crystal-white *gown* that *girl* unicorn-maidens wore... and he had it belted close with the usual cloth-of-gold sashy thing... and he'd manfully resisted the urge to trim his hair back to his usual length...

In other words, he was more or less *(really a lot more than less)* dressed up like a girl so that they didn't have to deal with *arguments* and *complaints* from random strangers and so that the usual mystique of unicorn-maidens would cover – and hopefully *protect* – them both.

Them *all,* but their other companion, the fairy-prince *(and commonly acknowledged King of the Pranksters)* Puck had needed to make a side-Quest to inform the Fairy Queen *(his Aunt... sort of)* about an impending invasion of the Fairy Wood *(and all the worlds it connected)* by the Evil Wizard whose troops currently controlled this town.

Presumably the umbrella of protection of being a unicorn-maiden's companions would be useful to Puck as well, once he got back and all three of them *(and Twinklestar, and Thony's-now-Amanita's horse Silverfoot, and Puck's fairy-mare, Chhilabiaen)* got back on the road. It was supposed to be several weeks or a month's ride to Puck and Amanita's homeland, a country named Pathremir, of which Thony knew absolutely nothing except that it was in the mountains and ruled by a matriarchy.

"People usually underestimate *me,* too," the new girl was saying. She wasn't more than a hair's-breadth taller than Amanita and had similar dark eyes and coffee-colored skin. "Maybe not *that* guy, though," she added thoughtfully, pointing back in the direction she had come from.

The greasy-seeming horse-dealer from earlier in the morning was bearing down on them, his face furious. He was a skinny little dude, so that would have been alarming, but not particularly so... but the huge bear of a guy following on his heels – and clearly at his direction – was rather more alarming.

Amanita's gaze narrowed as she looked between the new girl and the new arrivals. Thony could practically see the wheels clicking into place in her devious mind, so he wasn't surprised when his friend squared her shoulders and stepped between the angry men and the girl.

"What's the matter here?" she demanded, using a hand to fend off the greasy horse-dealer as he tried to reach around her to grab the new girl. The big guy stopped a few feet back and folded his arms, apparently trying to look intimidating. *(And, it had to be said, succeeding pretty well.)*

"That *girl* just released all me stock," the greasy guy snarled. "She's goin' t'pay for this trouble!"

Amanita looked over her shoulder. "Did you really do that?"

The girl shuffled her feet and looked down – to hide a self-satisfied smirk, Thony rather thought. "Eh... heh-heh-heh-heh-heh," she chuckled uncomfortably, but didn't deny it.

The young prince looked at the girl, feeling torn between being impressed and dismayed. Had she done it on purpose after seeing the state of those poor animals? He'd seen no solutions himself to their plight... not that he was sure that being released and then chased down would actually *improve* the situation for any of the beasts. But at least she had tried.

"I've had to hire a half-dozen louts t'track them all down," the fellow was ranting. "It's costin' me a fortune, and I'll never make 't all back! So that girl's a-going to pay me back instead!"

"But I don't have any money," the girl protested.

"Then I'll take it out o' yer hide!" the man growled.

They were starting to draw a crowd, Thony noticed nervously. All those fine people on their busy errands and their noses stuck in the air who'd been too busy to notice even a *unicorn-maiden* wandering around the town were far more interested when said unicorn-maiden seemed to be involved in an altercation in the middle of the street. A passel of kids in ragged clothing seemed to be arguing over something and exchanging money as they watched. At least none of the soldiers that he and Amanita had seen patrolling about in sharp-looking blue-and-black uniforms had yet been attracted.

"'Nita…" he began warningly. She had told him earlier not to use her full name; it was part of the reasons that she hadn't wanted him to know the name of her homeland, apparently, though she still wouldn't say *why*.

But she clearly didn't want anyone paying attention to them much more than he did.

Amanita heaved a great, put-upon sigh.

"Alright. I'm going to offer you a deal," she told the greasy horse-dealer. "You leave the girl alone and I'll buy one of your beasts. For any *fair* price you name."

The greasy-looking man calmed down slightly and gave the ex-stablegirl a speculative look. "Ye're the one was out to look at them earlier. I think ye had a few harsh words about the quality of me merchandise – likely an that ye didn't have coin to actually *buy* anything."

Amanita rolled her eyes. "I have coin. I'll take that donkey we looked at last."

The man settled his hands on his hips and gave her a crafty look. "And doubtless ye want a deal, because he'll be exhausted after runnin' 'round the city. I think ye're in league wi' *that* one." He jutted the scraggly hairs of his beard at the girl standing behind Amanita.

"I doubt the donkey – or any of the rest – went very far," Thony's companion commented. "None of them looked like *running* was a thing they were even capable of *doing*. I'll bet you got them all rounded back up even before you tried to chase her down. How many of them even tried to leave the paddock anyways?"

The man *harrumphed* a little. "That don't hardly matter. She messed with me business. And I *still* say yer in cahoots with 'er."

"I've never seen her before in my life. I just don't like your attitude," Amanita pointed out with some asperity. "Do you want to make a sale or not? I have other places I can buy from. And I *wasn't* planning on coming back to *you.*"

The fellow *hemmed* and *hawed* a bit more, but finally quoted Amanita a price for the worn-out donkey that made her wince. She counted out half the money right there, promising the second half when she came by that afternoon to get the donkey. The horse-trader and his goon went off satisfied, and what was left of the crowd began to disperse. Most of the ragged-looking kids looked disappointed, but a boy in a dirty green cap regarded Thony and his companions thoughtfully before turning and vanishing back into the flow of foot-traffic, the other kids following him.

"Well," the new girl said brightly. "That was a close one. Thanks, by the way. I guess I'll see you around."

"Waitaminute." Amanita grabbed at her arm as the girl seemed ready to dart off again. "You aren't going anywhere. You *owe* me, sister. *Big* time."

Thony didn't think Amanita had meant the word as anything other than a convenient way to refer to the other girl. But once she said 'sister' it was impossible not to notice the resemblance between the two girls.

Maybe this *was* some relation and that was why Amanita had stepped up to rescue her.

"Who are you anyhow?" Amanita demanded as the girl squeaked again about not having any money.

Okay, so maybe they *didn't* know each other.

"Dae Goldeneyes, mercenary extraordinaire at your service." The girl sketched a florid bow that was rather impeded by Amanita's grip on her arm and the way she had to grab for her bow to keep it from sliding off of her again.

Amanita reclaimed her hand and set her fists on her hips.

"*You're* Dae Goldeneyes?" she said in a tone of utter disbelief.

"Yup," the new girl said cheerfully. She looked at Thony. "Give me a hand with these arrows, dude?"

Thony blinked in surprise, but bent gamely to help her start collecting the scattered arrows. Yellow shafts banded with violet and fletched in orange and scarlet – he'd never seen such gaudy arrows. Not to mention that those weren't arrowheads for hunting, they were for warfare. It surely wasn't possible that a girl as small as 'Dae' could be a mercenary warrior – but her arrows and that huge sword on her back suggested otherwise.

"Dae Goldeneyes is a legend," Amanita stated bluntly, watching as Thony picked up arrows and the new girl checked the fletchings before putting them back in her quiver one by one. "The youngest mercenary ever to graduate from Sonoro's School of Soldiering. She's, like twelve or something."

Thony looked up with a frown. "A *school* for soldiers? And it let a *twelve-year-old* leave as a graduate? What kind of wack-a-doodle place is this?"

"I'm a child prodigy," Dae informed him a little primly. "There was no need for me to stay when I'd learned all they could tech me."

"*I* heard she was such a disaster that it was a delicate way of getting rid of her," Amanita said dryly. "The Iana warrior I traveled with for a few months told me that there were bets on in the Mercenaries' Guild about whether she'd survive the first month."

"Well, it's been almost three years," Dae said cheerily. "So, I guess that's pretty good."

"*You're* a *mercenary?*" Thony was boggled.

"Best one out there," Dae averred.

"Has anyone actually *hired* you for anything?" Amanita inquired.

"Of course." Dae contrived to look offended.

Amanita raised her eyebrows as Thony handed Dae the last arrow and stood up, brushing dust off his skirts. Not that they needed it; the fabric of the unicorn-maiden gown seemed to repel dirt and dust.

"Okay, not for awhile," Dae hedged, squirming a little under Amanita's gimlet gaze. "But I *have* been hired a few times. Mostly as a bodyguard for, like, royal kids and stuff. But they were *real* jobs."

"And they paid *real* money?" Amanita inquired. "That you don't happen to have anymore?"

Dae sighed. "I used it up. It's... been a little while."

Thony frowned. "Did the kids get assassinated or something? Why aren't you still doing the bodyguard thing?"

"The kids are just fine," Dae informed him. She winced. "I... well... see there was an accident... and I... kind of tripped on a duchess' skirt. At, like, a really important royal event. And it... kind of ripped off."

Thony winced.

"And... her petticoats kind of went with it," Dae went on. "And she had on this *really* skimpy underwear. And she'd had the king's name tattooed on her butt... in a heart... and..."

Amanita waved her to stop, one hand covering her eyes. "Please. Stop. Just... stop."

"It wasn't my fault," Dae averred.

"Uh-hunh," Amanita said skeptically. "And I suppose letting all of that guy's horses and things out of his paddock wasn't your fault either."

Dae gave her a wide-eyed look. "*I* just went inside to pat one of the horses that looked sad. How was *I* supposed to know that the latch was old and it wouldn't close properly? And then when the guy saw me in there and got mad and started yelling at me, is it *my* fault if I got freaked out and startled all the equines? And that one of them pushed on the gate and the latch opened up and then *they* all got out?"

"Yes," Amanita said.

"It was a good try, though," Thony said with more sympathy. "I wanted to do something to help them, but I couldn't think of anything."

"Except this didn't really accomplish anything," Amanita pointed out. "Except for me to seriously overpay for a donkey to get you out of trouble."

"Yeah, why *did* you do that?" Dae asked. "I mean, it was nice of you and all, but I've never met you before." She paused. "Actually, I don't even know who you are *now.*"

Amanita ignored this rather broad hint about as effectively as she did Thony's hints about wanting to know *why* where she was from was such a Big Secret.

"I felt sorry for you," the ex-stable girl said repressively. "My mother always said it's our place to help those who need aid." She glowered. "But you are totally *paying me back.*"

That... sounded a lot like Thony's lessons in Gallantry and Proper Princely Behavior.

Well, except for the end bit.

Dae began to ask how that was supposed to be any different from what the horse-trader had been threatening her with and Amanita was suggesting they could still switch things around and give Dae to the man and get her money back–

"I hate to break this up," Thony interrupted, "but a patrol of Raven troops just rounded the corner, and *no one* wants to get too close to them from what I've heard. Can we continue this conversation somewhere else? In our room back at the inn, maybe?"

"*Fine.*" Amanita gave Dae a last glower and began to stride off in a direction that Thony sincerely hoped would lead them back to the Inn of the Starred Hoof.

"*Fine.*" Dae glared back and flounced nonchalantly after her.

Thony sighed and started to trail after the pair of girls. Clearly they were two of a kind, and *one* Amanita was more than enough in his opinion.

He wasn't *quite* far enough behind to miss Dae 'whisper' loudly, "This redheaded dude looks like a girl in that dress. Does he know that?"

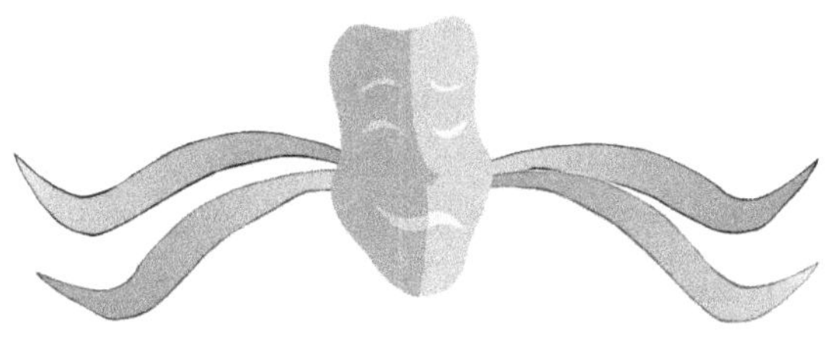

Chapter TWO

Secrets Don't Keep

A MINOR – AND SOMEWHAT irritated – negotiation with the innkeeper got them a room for Dae next door to their own and a third portion of lunch brought up to their room to share with her.

"You owe me for this, too," Amanita informed the – mercenette, Thony decided to consider her. She was too small to be a real mercenary. No matter what she said.

Dae shrugged. "Twice nothing is still nothing."

She tried to gnaw a bite of bread off, gave up and buried it in the grey-looking stew as the others had already done. She stared glumly at the unpalatable-looking mess. "Maybe I should be charging *you* for making me eat this."

"Don't even," Amanita told her. "Besides, Thony will eat up whatever you don't. *He's* still growing," she added dryly.

"I'm sure you're still growing, too." Thony gave the both of them a wary look. Dae, he'd discovered the hard way, was even *more* sensitive about her small stature than Amanita. Part of their negotiations with the innkeeper had included a slab of raw meat from his cold pantry to put on Thony's left eye after Dae had socked it.

Which was pretty gross, but was apparently the only way to get something cold out here on the plains. There was always ice available back home in Aldyrwald – even in late Summer someone would go up to a mountain peak fairly regularly and bring ice back down for everyone to buy.

"Is that feeling any better yet, Thony?" Amanita asked. "I'm starting to run low on arnica tea to make compresses after all we've used on your riding muscles, but we can't really have a unicorn-maiden running around with a black eye."

"I need to get the rest of this story on why *he's* a unicorn-maiden," Dae commented, prodding her buried hard roll under its layer of stew. The spoon still made a tapping noise when she tapped it on the roll.

"It's not terribly complicated," Amanita said breezily. "I didn't want to be one, and Twinklestar needed a partner."

Dae looked at her like she could tell that wasn't the real story, then at Thony, who quickly looked down at his own 'food.' The whole situation was still rather more than mildly embarrassing.

After a moment, Dae shrugged. "Well, I suppose it makes sense to keep dressing like a girl. People can be so *weird* when things don't fit with how they expect them to be. And with all that long, red hair, you're pretty enough to make it work," she told Thony seriously.

He glared at her. "*Weird* like when someone claims to be a mercenary when she's all of *twelve?*"

"Yeah, his hair grows super-fast," Amanita agreed quickly, clearly trying to head off another fight.

"I'm fourteen-and-a-half now," Dae said, not taking umbrage.

That made Amanita give her a sharp look. "Fourteen and a half? I thought you were twelve when I – I mean, the last I heard."

"Two and a half years ago I was," Dae tilted her head and looked disappointed. "You haven't heard about my exploits since then?"

"You've done something besides strip noblewomen down to their skivvies at royal balls?" Thony sniped grouchily.

Dae's cheeks turned rose-colored. "It wasn't a ball. It was the formal introduction of the kid I was guarding to the princess he was being betrothed to."

Thony could just imagine that happening at home. It was... funny, but not pretty. He had a fair amount of empathy for the kid she'd been guarding.

"I've been out of touch," Amanita put in, apparently to drag the conversation back. "So, what *have* you done that I should have heard about?"

Dae slouched down in her chair. "Not a lot, actually. Like you guys pointed out, there's not a huge number of people willing to hire someone my age as a mercenary."

In the awkward silence that followed, they all ate what they could of the stew and bread and Amanita started a fire and started a small pot of water heating to make the compress for Thony's eye.

"I... guess I'll go take a nap," Dae said at last. "Thanks for getting me the room. And, um, the 'food'."

Amanita nodded and the mercenette went out of their room.

"So, explain to me *why* you got her a room and all," Thony complained as Amanita soaked a rag in the arnica tea and squeezed out the excess water.

"Think about it, Thony," Amanita said without looking up from her work. "We're in the middle of a war-zone, in an occupied town. Neither of us have any real training in how to protect ourselves–"

"Speak for yourself," Thony muttered as she took the meat out of his hands and made him lie down so she could put the compress on his eye. "I was training with Roger and Jeremy for *months.*"

"And I traveled with an Iana warrior for a couple months myself," Amanita said reasonably. "She gave me lessons every day. But I still don't think I'm up for facing a whole army."

"We aren't supposed to be '*facing*' anyone," Thony pointed out. "Puck told us to stay here and in this room. He said if we don't go out, we should be safe."

Last night, after Puck had left them, Thony had been infected with Amanita's enthusiasm for figuring out what was going on by sneaking around the town and eavesdropping from actual eaves. If nothing else, the plan had the advantage of giving him an excuse not to wear the stupid dress, since he clearly couldn't climb around in such a thing.

Today, however, he'd gotten a glimpse of how big Flowerdust was... and the whole project seemed insane.

His eyes were closed, but he could practically hear Amanita rolling her eyes. "Even Puck didn't expect us to stay in here, Thony. Not *really.* I mean, he *knows* us."

There was no particularly good answer to that.

"So, you want to keep this Dae-person around to serve as *our* bodyguard?" Thony asked skeptically. "Isn't she sort of too accident-prone to make this a good idea?"

That gave her pause.

Or maybe she was just thinking about how to tell him that *she* was making this decision.

"I have to go get that stupid donkey," Amanita said after a minute.

Thony started to sit up. The morning had exhausted him and he was ready for a nap, but he wasn't going to let her go out there alone...

Amanita shoved him back down onto the bed. "Stay here. You need to keep that compress on your eye."

"You shouldn't go out there alone," he fretted. "Not with all those soldiers wandering around."

"I'll take Dae with me," she told him blithely.

"Great," Thony muttered, unreassured.

But he muttered it to empty air. Amanita had already gone.

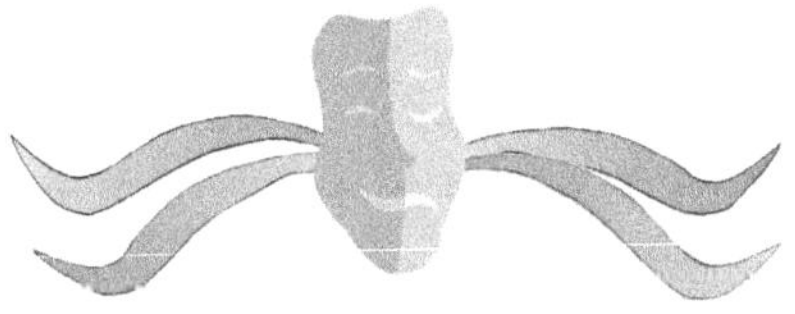

"I don't see what you needed me to come along for," Dae grumped as they walked back to the horse-trader. "This would probably go better if that horse-dealer guy and I *don't* see each other again."

"I agree completely," Amanita said.

"And I'd just started my nap."

"In the room *I* paid for."

"I *said* 'thank you'."

"And *I* said you'll pay me back. Which you're doing by going with me to the horse-trader."

Dae sucked her breath in through her teeth. "Okay. And then we're square?"

"Not by half," Amanita told her sweetly. "Besides, I thought you were a bodyguard by trade."

"I'm a *mercenary,*" Dae corrected her. "Bodyguard was just a job I had for awhile. And are you seriously going to tell me that you think you need a *bodyguard* to walk across *Flowerdust?* This is like the boringest place in the world. Nothing happens here."

"Nothing except *them.*" Amanita nodded discreetly at the latest patrol of Raven troops crossing the street ahead of them.

Dae shrugged. "They don't care about kids like us. We're no one important to *them.* We're not princes or princesses or anything." She grinned. "Of course, if you're *scared...*"

Amanita ground her teeth a little. "I'm not *scared.* I'm being *prudent.*" And it galled her to say it. Maybe she could blame it all on Thony. "Look, Thony's just been Chosen and as far as I know he's the only *boy* to *ever* have been Chosen a unicorn-maiden. So, we need to get him safely to the unicorn enclave in Selavan."

"He's a *unicorn-maiden,*" Dae pointed out. "No one is going to mess with him. Or with you, if you're with him."

"Who's going to believe he's a unicorn-maiden?" Amanita demanded.

"They'll kinda have to if the unicorn is with him," Dae told her. "Which brings me to another question. Why are the two of you staying in that shabby inn? If you can afford to bail me out of trouble, surely you could afford a better inn. And why stay in Flowerdust at all if you're so worried about *them?*" She pointed her thumb over her shoulder, now that they had turned onto a side-street to avoid the Raven troops.

22

"We're waiting for someone," Amanita admitted. "He left us here while he ran an errand and we have to wait for him to get back before we can leave. And... he warded our room, so we can't really move to a different inn. I don't think he realized how foul the place is," she added with some asperity.

"'Warded'?" Dae asked alertly. "Like with magick? *That* is pretty cool. So, your missing friend is a wizard or something? Ooooh," she went on. *"That's* why you're all worried. Those guys might be more interested in you than I thought. If you're involved with wizards and have a unicorn and all. Maybe you *do* need my help."

"Hmmn." That would do for now, Amanita decided.

They walked on for a couple more minutes as the mercenette mused over these ideas.

"Do I get paid?" Dae asked at last.

Amanita boggled at her. "You're kidding, right? I bailed you out by buying an overpriced, brokendown donkey I don't need and I'm paying for your room and board."

"That food sucks pretty badly," Dae noted.

"You said you had no money," Amanita reminded her. "So, you wouldn't be *eating* if I hadn't paid for it."

"Hmmn." Dae – whose eyes were not golden, all marketing aside – looked thoughtful. "There's more you aren't telling me."

"Obviously," Amanita agreed. "I just met you a couple of hours ago. In a hostile situation."

"But you're giving me a chance anyways," Dae pointed out. "And the way Thony says your name 'Nita,' it's an alias. I don't even know who the pair of you really are."

Amanita glared at her. "Do you want to pay for your own room?"

Dae held up her hands in a sort of mollifying gesture. "I'm just *saying...*"

"Don't. We're here." Amanita glanced at the other girl again. "*Try* not to get into any more trouble while I deal with our 'friend' here."

"He's a jerk who mistreats animals," Dae muttered rebelliously.

"Yeah, well, he's a jerk who can bring down the occupying troops on all our heads, so shut up and let me do the talking. And stay next to me with a stoic expression like a good little bodyguard."

"Who're you callin' 'little,' *Toots?*"

"I'm referring to the contents of your purse," Amanita said sweetly.

"Oh. Hmmn."

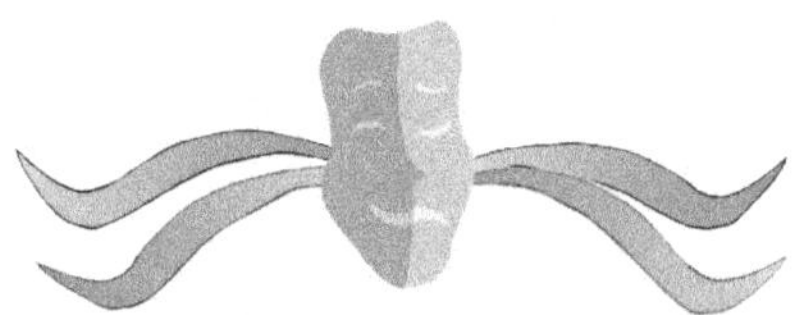

They retrieved the donkey with minor difficulty and Amanita resolutely pulled Dae away from the stockade. It had been refilled with the miserable-looking beasts... and another one was being returned as they finished their business, so it was obvious what 'skills' had been used to retrieve the horses and mules and donkeys.

This latest pony's head was hanging down in defeat, its ribs standing out against its heaving sides. It wasn't putting up any resistance, but the fellow bringing it in was snapping a whip over its head – and a thin trail of blood down the hindquarter facing where the two girls were watching attested to the fact that the whip had made contact at least once.

"We got this one away," Amanita muttered quietly to Dae as she exerted some real strength to pull the mercenette away from the scene. She'd learned early on that no matter what resources you had to throw at a problem... there were always more problems than you had the resources to solve. And right now, her resources were rather severely limited.

"It's not right, what he's doing to them," Dae muttered back. "I wish we could get them all away."

Amanita bit her tongue on the words that she wished *the same.*

"What would we do with an entire herd of half-starved equines?" she asked. "When Thony and I leave here, we're traveling over a thousand miles. I don't think most of those beasts could make it that far."

Dae shrugged. "I dunno. Let them go free out on the plains?"

Okay, so Amanita had agreed with the girl's soft heart over this. But not with her soft head.

"Those animals wouldn't last a month out there," she pointed out. "Most of them are sick or lame and that guy is hoping to sell them to people who don't know how to tell."

"Hunh." Dae looked dismayed... but still determined.

"The local wolves and vultures would be happy with your idea," Amanita added.

She had decided to protect the accident-prone mercenette on a whim – but now that she'd taken responsibility for Dae *(in one sense or another)* she had to make sure the girl didn't create *new* trouble. For *all* of them.

Dae looked like she wanted to argue, but was interrupted by a low chuckle from their right.

They both paused – the tired old donkey trundled on another couple of steps before realizing he could stop – and looked. Slouching against a wall of the alley to their right was a boy who looked close to their own age. He was dressed in dirty clothes that were somewhat less raggedy than many of the street-children Amanita had noticed as they wandered about, and he wore a dirty beret-style cap that might once have been a rather vivid green. He was turning a small pocket-knife around in his hands.

"You had a comment?" Amanita asked a bit sharply. He might be their own *age,* but under-sized as both girls were, he was a fair bit *larger.* She guessed the boy could look over the top of Thony's head, though he might not outmass the young prince, given how underfed he looked. Her friend Wes, who worked in the Aldyrwald Royal stables, was of a similar height but probably carried twice this boy's weight. In muscle.

"Saw you dealin' wi' ol' Styvan. Saw ye nerlier, too."

Dae rolled her eyes. "I'd think the whole *town* saw us."

The boy nodded genially. "Mebbe so. 'E's not a great favorite 'round here. Save for those as gets beasts from 'im when they needs 'un."

Dae pursed her lips and crossed her arms. "As bad as he is."

The boy nodded again. "Aye. So they are. Like to beat a lad as a horse, most of that type. Or a lass." He jutted his chin at the girls. "But *ye're* diff'rent. Ye stood up to Styvan and made it work out the way *ye* wanted it to. I was takin' bets," the boy added. "Nerlier. When Styvan was fairin' t'take the extra work outta yer hide." He looked at Amanita. "Mighta thought it'd be that 'corn-girl wit' ye would've stepped in, seems like the kinda thing they do. But 'twas ye. And ye're near as wee as this lass here."

Amanita grabbed Dae's arm again before the mercenette could make them more trouble with her rather vigorous *(and erroneous)* defense of her height. "What's your point, dude?"

"Los' me a fair bitta cash there," the boy told her. "Me an' a bunch o' others, though since I was the one makin' book, I still made a bit. Louris is pleased wit' ye, though. He always bets on the long shot. Usually loses him more'n it gains, but every now and then it works out. Like t'day."

Dae wrenched her arm back and planted her fists on her hips. "So, you're warning us that most of the other street-kids are annoyed with us? Thanks – *not*. We'll take it under advisement."

The boy shook his head. "Nay. There's one or two were o'erset for a bit, but I'll get 'em set straight. Thought at first ye knew 'chother from nerlier – but 'tis clear now 'tain't so. I like a lass as stands up for summun else 'gainst Styvan an' 'is type," he told Amanita straightly. "Jes'... wanted t'let ye know ye've been *seen*."

Amanita frowned at this. "'*Seen*'? What the heck does that mean?"

"Means ye *count* fer us, lass," the boy gave her a lopsided smile. "Means yer purse is safe here, by my word. Means we'll nip ye a word a trouble comin' for ye if'n there's need – and we'll 'spect ye'll do the same an ye see it comin' for a one o' us."

Amanita gave him a bemused look while Dae huffed about being the one who had released all the equines in the first place.

"Oh, we're lookin' at ye as well," the boy nodded to Dae. "And the 'corn-girl, too." He snickered. "Country-lass, is 'at one? Seemed hornswoggled by all the sights in the 'big city'."

"Hmmn." Amanita exchanged a look with Dae.

"Pretty thing, though, with that there hair," the boy noted.

"Hmmn," was all Amanita could manage again, though Dae seemed to be snorting to hide a fit of giggles.

"Ye're nae s'bad yerselves," the boy added with a hint of amusement, apparently interpreting their reactions as irritation that he hadn't mentioned them. "Don' look so a-hungered the way most of us on the streets do. New to it, aye? Stick w' Jost an' I'll see ye're fine. Easier with the fine weather comin' on now," he added thoughtfully. "Farmers don't take quite such a fit o'er a lost potato or pear an they know they'll be haulin' the half of 'em home at the end o' the day. Nor's it so bad sleepin' outta housen when Winter's nae breathin' down yer pants."

"Um... how'd you know?" Amanita stomped on Dae's foot to get her to keep her mouth shut. "That we're on our own, I mean."

He shrugged. "Ye've the look of it. And we've been watchin.' No adults wit' ye, and ye keep yer purse on yer belt instead o' inside yer clothes. Stayin' at t' Starred Hoof – where no one does an they aren' down on their luck and ekin' out the last bit o' coin till they give up an' live on t'streets."

"Hmmn." Amanita still wasn't sure what to say. She couldn't speak for Dae's appearance – clean if a bit threadbare and slightly outgrown – but she hadn't thought she and Thony looked so bad.

"The 'corn-girl didn' make no sense at first," Joss went on after a moment. "But seein' ye defend this lass, it's clear ye found the poor thing wandererin' and are settin 'er on 'er proper way. S'ppose her 'corn found 'er out on some Gods-forsaken farm sum'ere and she don't know the next-first thing 'bout gettin' 'erself where she belong. Sumplace where there's lots o' 'er kind." He sounded somewhat regretful.

"Um, yes..." Amanita half-agreed. "There's a place... up in Selavan. I think that's the plan."

"But *ye'll* be stayin' on *'ere,*" Jost said as if it was all settled. "Ain't nowhere near enough t'here for a kid down on 'er luck and with no'un t'look after 'er to make it to. Always glad to pick up new 'uns as already know to keep a friend's backside safe." He straightened up from his slouch. "Lemme know when ye're ready t'sell that fancy lookin' 'orse ye 'ave in the Starred Hoof's stables. And ye, when ye're lookin' t'pawn them weapons. Gods know there's a market fer both, wit' all these new sojers runnin' round, but I kin git ye a better price."

Amanita stomped on Dae's foot again before the outraged look could turn into a squeal.

"We'll think on it," she promised.

Jost laid a finger aside of his nose and gave one short nod before looking at Dae directly. "Might be ye should leave that stuff where folks won't see it, lass. There's those as will assume it's all yers and fairly won – and seek to try ye on't. And others as'll assume 'taint and seek to take it from ye w'ou' askin' nice. Cain't do ye nae good neither way."

Dae folded her arms and glared.

Jost chuckled. "Wall... done my best t'warn. Up to ye what ye do wit' the word. Remember me to yer friend, aye, lassies? Don' s'ppose she'd be up for walkin' out a bit? The 'corn-girl," he said in a reminding tone as they both stared at him. "She with that blaze o' bright hair."

"Ummmm..." Amanita's tongue seemed frozen.

Dae gave an exaggerated sigh. "I'm afraid not. They call them unicorn-*maidens* for a reason, you know. She's awfully snippety about the whole thing, and the unicorn is even *worse*. Their horns are sharper than spearheads," she added in a fake-confiding tone.

"Ah," Jost sounded disappointed but understanding. "Well. Imagine she'll be on 'er way right soon anyhoo. Them magick-types look after 'chother, soon or late."

"Yes," Dae blithered on. "I think she said she's waiting for someone who's supposed to meet her here in Flowerdust. Isn't that right, Nita?"

Amanita nodded without adding anything. This was... just too bizarre.

Jost cocked his green cap jauntily. "Well. I'll be seein' ye around then. Any'un else talks to ye, ye tell 'em ye'll be on Jost's crew an the day comes, aye?"

"Uh, sure," Amanita mumbled as Dae elbowed her sharply in the ribs.

Jost grinned. "Little things like ye... keep those sweet faces and we'll have work for ye both for a good long time. Ain't no one'll say 'no' an a pretty little thing comes up a-beggin'. Nor like to think 'tis the precious li'l chil' as slipped the coin outta their purse – but they'll be shamed when a search of the great honkin' lad they fingered as a thief comes up with nothin' but the 'oles in 'is pockets. Might e'en gi'e that 'poor, wronged lad' a copper for his troubles," he added with a wink.

And with that, Jost turned and sauntered off down the alley.

Amanita and Dae looked at each other.

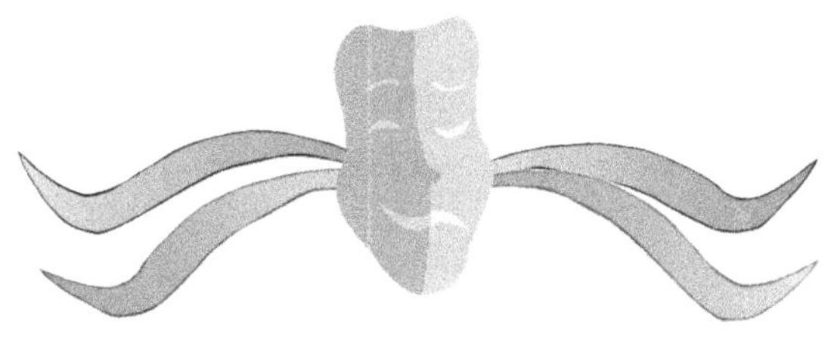

Chapter THREE

Puck, the Magick Prankster

"**W**HAT JUST HAPPENED?" THONY DEMANDED as the girls tried to relate the tale of Jost and his... job offer.

Or rather, as Amanita did.

Dae was... um... *literally* rolling on the floor laughing.

And they hadn't even gotten to the part yet about Jost trying to ask Thony out on a date. Possibly she was laughing pre-emptively.

Amanita glared at the mercenette. "Go get your own dinner. I need to talk to Thony."

Dae snickered. "About *what*, I wonder."

But she went.

Amanita locked the door behind her with a sigh of relief. "Everything is harder with that girl around."

"But we're *keeping* her around," Thony commented dryly. There was a little bit of greenish-yellow discoloration around his eye, but the arnica had clearly done its job. "Because she's going to be an effective *bodyguard.*"

Amanita leaned her head forwards and rested it on the locked door. "Thony..."

There was a gusty sigh from behind her. "Nevermind. I liked her attitude about the horses, too. And her moxy. It wouldn't have occurred to me to try just letting all those animals free."

The girl straightened up and turned around with a wry grin. "I guess you're just too well-behaved. Me, too," she added as his eyebrows reached for his hairline. "Actually, *that's* why we need her the most. Social norms don't seem to inconvenience Dae the way they do you or me."

"Hunh." But Thony didn't really seem to disagree. "When do you suppose our latest ration of indigestibl–"

There was a knocking, and Amanita opened it to admit the little kid with their tray. *He* was clean and dressed in well-made, if simple clothes, Amanita noted, contrasting him to Jost and the street-kids she'd glimpsed here and there. And he looked well-nourished as well. Clearly the money the innkeeper was making off his guests was going to at least some good use.

Thony was glowering at the food and seemed on the verge of saying something...

"The innroom seemed pretty full last night," Amanita remarked to the kid as he set the tray down and before Thony could open his mouth. "Is the beer better than the stew?"

The little boy reddened a bit and kept his eyes on the work of arranging their utensils rather more carefully than necessary. "So I'm told."

The girl snorted slightly. Meadowmouse, the Iana warrior she had traveled with, had made her more aware of some of the economics of travelers' inns. "And mugs don't need much more than a rinse and wipe. And beer mops up easier than stew. And with just beer, he can probably keep you in the back and handle the taproom on his own."

The boy lifted his eyes to meet hers with a startled expression. "And my mum and my sister. No one ever asks for a second bowl of stew. Are you an innkeeper's daughter?"

Amanita shook her head. "No, someone just explained this stuff to me... a long time ago."

Her glance met Thony's, and he looked a little chagrined.

The little boy looked torn. "We have better food for the family – and that minstrel-lady, so she'll stay around longer. Papa says people fight less when there's music."

"And I'll bet they buy more beer, too," Amanita suggested.

"Yeah," the boy admitted. "They spill more, so they buy more. Happy songs, and they toast each other and it sloshes everywhere. Sad ones and they blubber into their drinks and their mugs tip over and they need refills. It's a mess to clean up the next morning, but the coinbox is full."

He seemed to make up his mind. "You seem to be staying here for awhile. And you already figured it out. I'll ask Mama to let me bring you real food."

Thony looked like the sun had just come out from behind clouds.

Amanita grinned. "Thanks. Do we need to, like, swear to secrecy about your mother's cooking skills or something?"

The boy shook his head shyly. "Naw. Jost says you're good for that sort of thing."

He was out the door before Amanita could ask a follow-up question.

"Jost, hunh," Thony was already working on burying his roll in the stew to soak it soft enough to gnaw on. "That's the kid who's ready to help you and Dae live on the streets."

"You, too," Amanita retorted. "He just doesn't think you'll be here long enough. Since you're a 'magick-type person'." Was this the time to mention...?

Thony snorted. "Whatever. We're going up on the rooftops tonight, right? I assume our main target will be that really big building with the wall around it?"

"The mayor's mansion?" Amanita considered it. "Yeah, that makes sense. I think I heard someone say that the Raven troops have taken it over and made it their headquarters. So, there's a good chance we'll overhear something interesting there."

"I hadn't realized that they'd done that." No, it wasn't her imagination that Thony had gone a little pale. His freckles were almost invisible most of the time, but they stood out now.

For a moment, the girl wondered if he was going to back out of the plan.

For a moment... she kind of hoped he would...

But the run of emotions across his face suggested that Thony was remembering that *she* was willing to do this. And that she was 'just' a girl. And younger than him.

She saw him look down as if to avoid meeting her gaze... and that was the kicker, because it made him look at the unicorn-maiden gown...

"What are we going to do with Dae while we're out eavesdropping?" Thony asked. "Or are we inviting her to come along?"

That idea made Amanita wince. The idea of the accident-prone mercenette involved in such a delicate undertaking seemed... fraught.

"We're not going out till it's dark and everything, right? So, she should be asleep by then."

Thony gave her an odd look. "Hiring a bodyguard and then leaving her behind while you go off to do dangerous things seems a little..."

"Wise, in this case?" Amanita suggested.

"Dumb, in general?" Thony shot back.

The girl rolled her eyes and stacked their dishes back on the tray. "Do *you* want her to come along?"

"Not really," Thony replied, picking up the tray and taking it to over to the door so he could leave it in the corridor for the innkeeper's son to collect.

When he opened the door, however, there was Dae. She looked up at him perkily, then peered around him at Amanita.

"What did he do when you told him about Jost wanting to take him on a date?"

Thony's head whipped around to look at Amanita and he nearly lost control of the tray and all its breakable items. Dae tried to stabilize it for him and mostly succeeded in tripping over his feet and sprawling halfway across the threshold.

Thony managed to set the tray and its contents out in the hallway, drag the mercenette into the room, and shut the door before he exploded.

"*AMANITA!*" he cried furiously. "*What the HELL?*"

"Ooops," said Dae, from the floor. "I guess you didn't tell him. *Nita.*"

She was giving Amanita an odd look, so the former stablegirl guessed there was no real chance Dae hadn't heard exactly what Thony had called her. Nor that *she* didn't know exactly who Amanita was.

Given how *loud* Thony was being, this whole incognito thing might be out the window anyways.

"Thony, shut *up,*" Amanita ordered him.

"Puck said he spelled the whole room so no one will even notice us here," the boy pointed out, still fuming. "That would hardly work if people could hear us talking, so clearly he made sure no one *could.*"

Which made a great deal of sense, actually. Thony seemed to have a really good grasp of what and how magick could be used when he put his mind to it.

Well, that and other things, too. After all, he was just as well-educated as Amanita was herself... a fact it would do her good to remember. Just because he wasn't familiar with this new venue – her world and an urban setting more generally – didn't mean he wasn't just as quick-witted, observant, and thoughtful as he'd been back in Aldyrwald.

"Fair enough," she agreed. "And, I'm sorry, I should have told you. There just didn't seem to be a good opportunity to bring it up. Jost thinks you're really a girl – he didn't get a particularly good look at you, I guess."

"This is the sort of thing you *make* an opportunity for." Thony looked like he was trying to decide if that was a compliment or an insult. "I mean, what if I end up running into this guy?"

"Oh, it shouldn't matter," Dae chirped from the floor. "I reminded him that unicorn-maidens have to stay, you know, *maidens.*"

Thony's cheeks now tried to match his hair, and Amanita hastened to add, "He thinks you're leaving shortly anyways. He has this impression that I'm some sort of do-gooding Samaritan who's just lost her parents and that I'm helping you out while you wait for someone to get here and help you go off to Selavan."

She rolled her eyes to emphasize the absurdity of that idea.

"Don't dis it," Dae opined. "Who knows if this Jost-kid will come in handy while we're all here." She gave them a smug grin when the other two looked at her sharply. "Oh, come on. It's easy to see you two are up to something. That's why you brought me on, right? More allies can only be useful."

Thony groaned and sat down heavily on one of the beds, leaning over to put his elbows on his knees and his face in his hands. "This is *not* getting better. Maybe we should actually do that. Just wait till Puck gets back and then high-tail it to this Selavan-place. Or to... your homeland."

He managed *not* to name Pathremir, which was a bit like closing the barn-door after letting the horses out, but it was a nice try. At least he'd remembered that much.

And it distracted Dae.

"Wait," the mercenette exclaimed. "That's the second time you've used that name. You don't mean the fairy prankster? *He's* your missing traveling companion?"

"Um, no?" Amanita hadn't really planned to share that part with Dae.

Unfortunately, Thony had shrugged in agreement, still staring rather miserably at the floor.

"He *is!*" Dae said gleefully, her eyes shining with excitement. "That is *so cool!* Are you two, like, his apprentices or something? Are you going to stop the sorcerer and his army with pranks?"

Thony looked up in alarm, and even Amanita had to take a step back at the other girl's enthusiastic fervor.

"Of course not..."

Not that it hadn't occurred to her to try. Nor to Thony either, she suspected – after all, it was an unparalleled opportunity to use their pranking skills for the Greater Good.

"You *are,*" Dae insisted. "I can tell! C'mon, guys, don't make me beg! I want in! I'm an awesome prankster, too!"

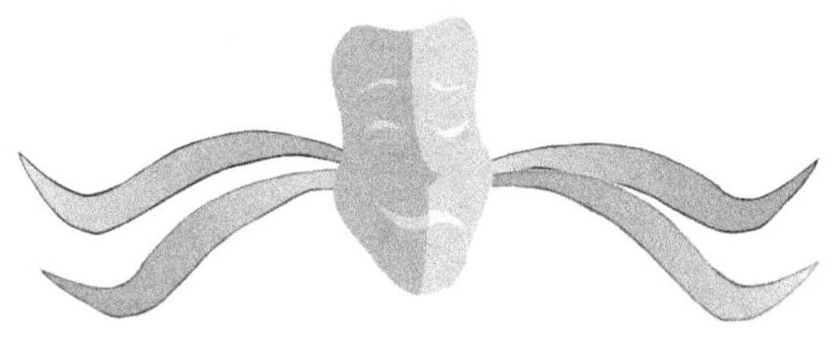

Chapter FOUR

I Spy with My Little Eye

IT TOOK A GREAT DEAL of fast talking to get Dae out of their room. Not off her crazy idea – Thony feared there was no real way to do that, and just had to hope that she wouldn't try to convince them to let her 'help' by beginning her own campaign of pranks.

At least even Amanita seemed to think this was absolute raving insanity.

Not that he doubted she'd considered the matter.

As he had himself, for all of three seconds.

Because it was *stupid,* and neither he nor Amanita were that dumb.

He hadn't thought Dae seemed to be either, but he'd known her for all of a handful of hours so his first impression might have been mistaken. At very lest the mercenette was impetuous, accident-prone, and volatile.

The young prince rubbed gently at the tender area around his eye that at least wasn't as discolored as it deserved to be. Thank the Gods for Amanita's handy little herb.

At least he'd be pretty for when that *street-kid* saw him next, Thony thought a little savagely. Damn this stupid dress!

"It's getting noisy downstairs," Amanita commented as she came away from the door after locking Dae out. "I mean *really* noisy."

"Didn't the innkeeper's boy say music keeps their customers from fighting?" Thony asked. "'*music doth sooth the savage beast,*' and all. I thought that minstrel was still here."

"I heard some music along with the rest of the noise," the ex-stablegirl replied. "I think she might be trying to help, but there's only so much music can do unless she's using magick... and that might not be the greatest idea in the world with the town occupied by a sorcerer's forces."

They could hear crashing sounds from below now, which either meant a full-blown bar-fight – or Dae was down there. Thony had seen a couple of Papa's knights attempt a duel – on the tabletops at dinner – when they'd had rather too much to drink. It had ostensibly been in relation to the attentions of one of Mama's ladies-in-waiting... Papa had dismissed both knights the next day and sent the lady in question back to her father's holding, since she'd seemed rather too pleased to be the object of contention. *(Thony had heard that the young lady's father had encouraged her to set the two knights a set of three Tasks when they followed her home – just as if she were a princess, though at least she **was** his only child. It hadn't gone well. One of the knights had headed off on his Task, but the other had turned around once he was sure the other fellow was well-gone and then demanded the young lady's hand – by holding her father at swordpoint. The lord – one of Aldyrwald's vassal-*

barons – had protested to Papa, as had his daughter's other suitor. But King Bill's hands had been tied, since by then it was obvious that the baron's daughter was soon to be a mother. At least she hadn't seemed terribly displeased with the outcome...)

"Hmmn." Thony looked at Amanita speculatively. "You're curious about what's going on down there, too. There's a loose floorboard... I noticed it squeaking when Puck was pacing around last night. And I tested it when you were out."

He went over and pried the board up out of the floor. It left a gap of some four inches by three feet, and gave them a clear view straight down over the minstrel's head.

The woman had withdrawn into her niche by the hearth, her stringed instrument *(it was one Thony wasn't familiar with)* hugged tight to her rather ample bosom. Apparently, she'd given up trying to soothe the savage beasts.

Beyond her, it wasn't a great angle for the kids to see the rest of the inn. But by moving carefully around the gap, it was possible to get a glimpse of chairs being used as blunt weapons and see other, smaller items flying through the air. There was also some rather foul language being shouted.

"If they don't stop this, one of the neighbors is likely to forget the town is occupied and try to call the local constables," Amanita muttered to Thony.

He winced at that thought. *"That's* not likely to go well..."

She shook her head in agreement.

That wouldn't be good for the pair of *them* either. How far Puck's protective spells would go, Thony couldn't begin to guess.

Suddenly Amanita groaned softly. It was very quiet, especially compared to the furor in the taproom, but the minstrel below them seemed to cock an ear and they both froze. Silently, Amanita pointed out the reason for her noise.

Just barely visible from their floorboard gap was, unmistakably, the drifting tails of the red-and-gold armband on Dae's upper left arm. She'd told them proudly that the triple-wrapped scarf was proof-positive of her membership in the Mercenaries' Guild.

Thony put a hand up to rub at his temple. The slight headache that had remained after the mercenette had punched him earlier, and despite all the rest and treatment, was beginning to bloom into something rather more painful.

Amanita's expression was sympathetic... and rueful.

They didn't have so much as a moment to wonder if they should go down and try to extract the other girl from the situation, however, because suddenly there seemed to be Raven troops everywhere *(or as much as they could see)*, given the flashes of their distinctive and vivid blue jackets as they moved around. The room had gone silent.

"Good thing my patrol and I were passing by," a man's cultured voice said genially. A light voice, and casual... but it was underlain with tension.

More silence.

"Thank us for dealing with your drunks, innkeeper," the same man's voice ordered. "My men and I are thirsty, and I hear the beer you serve here in mugs is better than the swill you offer in bowls." He paused. "You there, musician. Play something lively."

The woman directly below them stepped out of her niche slightly and settled herself down on the stool she must have abandoned during the fight. Her fingers began to trill along the strings in a feisty tune.

Dae seemed to have gone unnoticed.

Thony and Amanita heaved a *(silent)* sigh of relief and the boy was actually starting to lift the floorboard in order to replace it, when one of the Raven soldiers came right up to the minstrel as she played.

They froze again, looking at each other. It was one thing if the minstrel noticed some noise above her – she'd likely dismiss it as rats or something. A soldier was likely to be much more suspicious.

And... the soldier – all they could see of him from this angle was a head of highly-styled black hair – had now put an arm around the woman playing the instrument. His other held a full mug of beer, the froth seemingly undisturbed since it had been pulled from the keg. The hems of his garments were touched with thin silver-braid.

"Julanna," he said, and it was the same voice who had commanded the innkeeper to serve him and his men, but the tension had more than doubled. "She'll be here any moment. It was all I could do to get here ahead of her..."

"It'll be fine, Istevan," the minstrel murmured. Her voice was clearly that of a trained speaker, and she sounded more amused than worried. Her fingers didn't miss a note. "You can still manage your part?"

"*I* can. It still seems chancy to me. Davril and Daphne are still upstairs?"

"Hey, Lieutenant," came a voice from out of sight. "You going to let that girl of yours actually *sing?*"

"Now, Corporal, we'll have to see about that. I might have better uses for these pretty lips than amusing you." A kind of lazy arrogance flooded back into the voice of the man below them. By the surprised squeak that the minstrel made, Thony surmised that the soldier's fingers had gone in an unexpected place. Amanita's face had darkened, possibly at the man's presumption.

"You'll have her all the night, Lieutenant. She's got the best songs in this dirty little town. Can't she give us a song first?"

"Oh, so it's a *dirty* little song you want, Corporal?" The minstrel laughed and looked up at the man with his arm around her. "Surely there's time for a dirty *little* song, Lieutenant?"

The Lieutenant heaved what sounded – to Thony – like a patently faked sigh of annoyance. "Fine. But just the one. Up you get, girly." And he made the woman get up and then resettle herself in his lap.

"Taking this a little *far,* aren't you, Istevan?" The minstrel's voice was just barely audible to the two young people listening from above over the sound of her testing the tuning of her strings.

"You wanted to put on a *show,* Julanna." The man's face was buried in the musician's tumbled red-gold curls, but his tone was grim. "*I* wanted you and Dav and Daphne out of here, if you'll recall."

"I wouldn't be very good at my *job* if I cut and run the instant things got a little *interesting,* dear," came the reply as she began a very different chording.

"Your *job* is to play music," the man complained, as the woman began to sing. "This... is just a temporary thing."

"A fairy-lass was out one day,

O'er the hills and far away,

Dressed in her fairy-best to play..."

Amanita was tugging Thony back from the gap in the floorboards and trying to wrest the missing one out of his grasp, so he lost the next few phrases. Her face was flaming, which made him both more curious about the song and about how she knew it was so terrible.

Their silent wrestling match took a great deal of his concentration, but another wisp of music distracted him.

"...and she fluttered on down to the willow-grove,

O'er the hills and far away,

From you or I that fine bright day,

And the knight, he was bent upon meeting her there..."

"Cut it out," Thony hissed as she managed to get the board away from him.

"You do not want to hear the rest of that," Amanita whispered back, furiously. "It's *not* a nice song at all, and certainly not meant for kids to hear."

"Well, *Dae* is," he pointed into the gap where the ditty had reached a chorus, and Dae's voice was clearly audible over all the heavier, adult ones.

Amanita turned an even brighter shade. "She's a *mercenary.* That's completely different from people like you and me. We're held to a higher standard than listening to... to..."

"Why?" Thony asked, only half paying attention as he tried to catch more of the words.

"Because of who we *are,* you nincompoop!"

He glanced up in surprise, wondering if he was finally going to get some of her backstory at last...

...and just then the music came to an abrupt halt. It wasn't a chorus anymore either, so it stopped all at once. He and Amanita exchanged a worried glance and put their faces as close to the gap as they could.

"When I heard you had a *girl* in the most tawdry tavern in town, Lieutenant," came a woman's drawl, "I was sure there must be an exaggeration going on."

Lieutenant Istevan's hand had apparently stilled Julanna's strings. Now he stood up abruptly, dumping the musician off his lap. She caught herself on the edge of the hearth, protecting her instrument by taking the risk of falling into the fire, and shot him a look of irritation that probably wasn't just for show.

The Lieutenant wasn't looking. He was saluting sharply.

"Captain. I..."

Another person came, just barely into view. "At ease, Lieutenant. Which you clearly *were.*"

The woman with the voice was slender, but moved with utter confidence as she looked disdainfully at the minstrel crouched on the floor over her instrument. She was wearing those ubiquitous sleeveless blue jackets over the same black pants and shirt, but there was even more silver braid at her hems than on Istevan's. Her hair was also black, like his, but instead of being over-styled into waves, it fell in a smooth, straight black curtain to an inch above her shoulders. Her skin was pale, as if she avoided the sun, though, whereas Istevan's – and Julanna's – had the healthy, golden glow of people who spent time out of doors.

"Captain," Istevan began again, a bit of a tremor in his voice. "Shalladra, I'm sorry..."

"Don't *unman* yourself before your troops, Lieutenant," the Captain drawled. She turned away. "Innkeeper. Your best ale for my men. *All* of my men. Not that that will be anything to write home about, I'm sure, but it's the best that can be managed in this one-horse town."

"Yes, Captain-Mayoress," they could hear the innkeeper answering obsequiously.

By squirming a bit, Thony could just barely see the Captain (*'Captain-Mayoress'? did that mean she was the commander of the Raven troops occupying Flowerdust?).* She accepted a frothy mug from the innkeeper and turned back around to face the room, leaning her elbows behind her on the bar. A certain amount of movement in the background suggested that there were more soldiers getting mugs a bit farther away – at the far end of the long bar that separated the beer from the customers, presumably. It seemed that no one wanted to come particularly close to the Captain when she was in a mood.

Hopefully Dae had made herself scarce before she was noticed.

"What a... truly tragic place for a man like *you* to end up, Lieutenant," the Captain noted, with bitter amusement. She had almost as beautiful a voice as that of the minstrel, Thony noted absently. He was moderately surprised that he could hear anything when she was no longer pitching her voice for the rest of the taproom's occupants. But if the minstrel had selected this corner to play in because it amplified her voice, perhaps it also did the same in reverse.

Lieutenant Istevan strode over to the Captain, hesitating as he came close as if he wasn't sure if he should salute or slip an arm around her. Or possibly fall at her feet and lick her boots.

Apparently, he settled on brazening it out. The lazily arrogant tone they'd first heard when he came over to the minstrel made a reappearance as he settled himself beside. "Shalladra... I have to find something to do when you're busy. And you're busy so *often.*"

The Captain tilted her head, her straight black hair falling aside to reveal the lower curve of her ear. "You're getting it wrong, Istevan."

Her eyes were fixed on the minstrel, who was now dusting herself – and her instrument – off and ignoring them both to all appearances. Thony didn't doubt that the musician could hear the quiet conversation even better than he could himself. A glance at Amanita showed that she was just as enthralled.

"I thought you liked it when your subordinates showed initiative, Shalladra."

"Not when it makes me look a fool, *Lieutenant*." The Captain's eyes raked Julanna-the-minstrel's well-endowed form. "I suppose it's obvious what *she* has that might bring you down to such a dive so regularly." She tore her eyes away and grimaced into her mug. "It certainly can't be the quality of – I don't even dare call it 'libations'."

"Free time," Istevan replied just as quietly. "That's all. You're running the whole operation here. I'm just a lowly lieutenant with too much time on my hands."

"Hunh. I'll have more *time* when milord gets here, but less *freedom* in how I spend it."

"And you'll be *so* disappointed about that." Istevan's tone had become... artistically unhappy. Even *petulant*. If Thony hadn't heard him talking to the minstrel before all this went down, he'd have believed it was real. "I'm not any more important to *you* than the minstrel is to *me*."

The Captain turned to look at him, and Thony caught a flash of eyes that were as bright a blue as his own. "Clever argument, Istevan. I might even buy it... if I hadn't seen the way you were looking at her when I walked in."

"Shalladra, there's nothing, I *swear*–"

"Don't forswear yourself, darling. I should be done with my work by the second hour after midnight. Make sure you're back by then." She reached up and patted his cheek rather condescendingly. "Have your fun while you wait up for me."

And with that, the Captain left her mug in Istevan's hands and strode out – collecting the soldiers she'd brought with her as she went, to judge by the sounds.

Istevan carefully set the mostly-full mug back on the bar and swallowed hard *(Thony could actually see his Adam's apple bobbing up and down)*. He looked at Julanna. The minstrel-woman was studiously ignoring him as she re-tuned her strings.

The man came back over to her. "Well, girly, are you going to finish that song, or shall we just head upstairs?"

To Thony's ear, it didn't sound so much like *arrogance* this time as *desperate bravado*. Judging by the way Amanita stiffened, though, *she* still heard it as arrogance.

The woman didn't look up. "Because your *mother* has given you her *permission*, little boy?"

Thony cringed. No way this was going to go well...

There wasn't anyone – besides the watchers in the ceiling – to see Istevan's wince. He certainly didn't let it show in his tone. "Getting uppity for a minstrel playing a tavern no better than she should, aren't you, girly?"

At the return insult to her musician's skills, Julanna's head jerked up in automatic response. She was blocked from being seen by the rest of the room, but her face was tilted up to Istevan's, so Thony could see her expression soften...

...just before the man scooped her up, instrument and all, and tossed her over his shoulder.

There were some approving jeers that must be coming from Istevan's men, as the pair vanished from view.

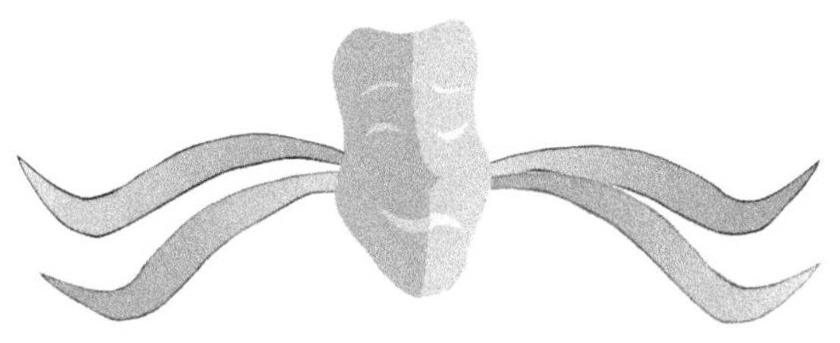

Chapter FIVE

The Lost Princess

D AE POUNDED URGENTLY ON THONY and Nita's – no, *Amanita's* – door. Thony opened it, and Dae – of course – fell into the room.

She pulled her feet in and gestured for him to close it, quickly.

"I don't want them to see me!" she squeaked. "I wouldn't have made it up the stairs before them, but he had to stop on the landing to set her down. Oh, wait..." The mercenette paused in dismay. "You don't know what just happened downstairs!"

"Actually, we do," Amanita told her and pointed at the loose board. "That one comes up. We could see and hear it all."

Dae came over to examine the floorboard. "Cool!"

Thony gestured them to hush. He'd left the door open a crack, and now he was listening carefully. The girls waited impatiently.

"It's all clear now," he said after a moment. "I think they went into the room just past ours."

He nodded to the appropriate wall behind the bed that he was using to sleep on, and Amanita immediately clambered onto it with one of the wooden tumblers in her hand to put against the wall.

Dae looked at them in amazement as Thony followed suit after closing and locking the door.

"Eeeewwww!" she exclaimed. "You guys are *gross*. Or do you even know what they're probably doing over there?"

Thony lifted his head to give her a *look*. "Puh-lease. We could hear everything they were saying. They are *not* doing what you're thinking."

Dae's eyes grew round, and she hunted around for another tumbler. Finally, she gave up and lined up with the other two, kneeling on the bed and with her ear pressed to the wall.

"–sn't supposed to happen this way."

"Calm down, 'Stev," a man's voice said firmly. "You're hyperventilating."

"No, I'm still trying to catch my breath. Julanna's no featherweight and I carried her half up the stairs." Istevan's voice.

A feminine chuckle. "Which was sweet, if rather thickheaded. Perhaps *we* should be worried about *you* if that's the limits of your acting abilities."

"*I* have Shalladra wrapped around my little finger," Istevan retorted dryly. "*I* could manage just *fine* if I wasn't having to worry about all of *you*."

The other male voice sighed. "At least you're out there *doing* something, both of you..."

"Davril..." Istevan's tone was mollifying. "Daphne needs you – and we *all* need you both to be safe."

"I know, I know. Let's just... get this whole business over with as soon as possible, okay?"

"Fine by me," Julanna again, and now her voice was almost crisp. "Have you found out anything about why they targeted Flowerdust? Is... *he* still out by Darjil?"

A pause. "No. I don't have as much time as I would like to go through Shalladra's papers, though, so it's possible I've missed something. I've been through all the official communiqués... three times each. There's nothing *there.*"

Julanna sighed. "We have to find *something.* Either he's coming here because the Fairy Wood is his ultimate target–" *(Dae noticed Thony look around in alarm)* "–or he's setting up for a thrust farther to the west. They sent *us* in because they thought that we were most likely to be able to figure this out."

Davril's voice, reluctant. "Because *you* were, you mean. Maybe we should have stuck to the original plan and let you be the one to go in."

Istevan snorted. "There were reasons that wasn't going to work from the beginning. *That* one, in particular–" he must have indicated something in the room, "–but it was also vanishingly unlikely that *Captain-Mayoress Shalladra Icicleblood–*" and his voice dripped with sarcasm, "would have let Julanna in close enough to search through her papers."

"She seems rather hotter than icicles when it comes to *you,* 'Stev." Davril's voice was... very dry.

"Davril..." And Istevan's was embarrassed.

"We all know why she ended up with that nickname," Julanna said dismissively, "and it had nothing to do with *that.* I wouldn't have tried to go through *her,* of course, I'd have done it the other way. I still *could...*"

"We're here now," Davril disagreed, "and Istevan is embedded in Shalladra's legion. We should work with what we've got going already, not jump in a new – and more dangerous – direction just because this is taking too long." A brief pause, and then he added, "More dangerous for *Daphne*, as well as you, Julanna."

The minstrel sighed. "Less so for the two of you, though."

"Well, for Istevan, anyways," Davril noted. "*I'm* just staying quietly in this room all day. I might be *bored* to death, but – mmphff!"

"I'm in no particular danger," Istevan corrected him after a moment's pause. "Not so long as I keep the Icicle Princess happy." He paused. "The rest of you, though... we can find another way for me to pass you the information I'm not finding. I'd feel better about all of this if we got you out of here. Where *he* can't find you."

"There's nowhere that safe," Julanna said a little sadly. "Not even now, and once *he* knows..."

"Saf*er* then," Istevan sounded somewhere between impatient and resigned. "Nevermind. I know you too well, Julanna Silversea. Simple good sense never did make you change your mind." He sighed. "I need to be getting back."

"It's nowhere near midnight yet, and she said she wanted you back *after...*" That was Davril's voice. He sounded disappointed.

A small snort. "And you didn't see that for the little loyalty test it was? Better for our *Plan* if I'm there long before midnight, when Her Captain-ness comes looking for me early."

The sound of a chair scraping on the floor.

"Do me a favor and *try* not to do anything that might give Shalladra an excuse to look at you for any *other* reason, please?" The sound of the door opening and closing.

"I might as well go back down and play a few more sets," Julanna said with a sigh. "The locals here don't seem much inclined to tip me – and by now *someone* has likely stolen the coins I seeded my tipping cup with – but I should make it look good. A down-on-her-luck minstrel who's willing to sleep with a local bullyboy to make ends meet wouldn't miss a chance to earn a few more pennies."

"'Down-on-her-luck'..." Davril made a strange noise. "They don't know what they're getting, having a full-fledged *Bard* to treat their ears."

A rich, musical laugh. "They don't, and hopefully they won't, if we're to make this work. It's a good thing these people have been cut off from news for so long or I'd have had to dye my hair as well as use a *nom de musique*. I'll see you in a few hours, Davril, dear."

The door opened and closed again.

And there was nothing else to hear except for a Davril releasing a long, frustrated-sounding sigh.

The three young people in the next room pried themselves off the wall and looked at each other.

"Well." Amanita said thoughtfully. "*Well*, well, *well*, well, *well.*"

Thony was rubbing the impression of the rim of the wooden cup out of his ear. "So, they're spies."

"*Well-connected spies,* it sounds like," Amanita pointed out.

"And they think the Fairy Wood might be in danger," Thony added, looking anxious.

Amanita waved this aside. "The Fairy Wood can defend itself. Puck is seeing to that. But if this Valderon Raven'sWing dude – and I assume that's the *'he'* they kept referring to – if he pushes his army farther west, that's where *my* homeland is."

Thony gave her a side-eyed look. "Didn't Puck say there's people over there whose whole job is to handle Evil Wizards?"

That was news to Dae.

Apparently, it wasn't all that familiar to Amanita either. "I'm not sure exactly *what* he said. I know about those people, but I've never heard they did anything like *that.*"

"Which people?" Dae asked brightly. She'd discovered years ago that acting all wide-eyed and innocent was effective at getting people to explain stuff to her. It worked better on adults – or even taller people, who thought she was a little kid – than on Thony and Amanita, but one used what one had.

The other girl pursed her lips. "I'm not sure I should say. I don't think Puck told us on purpose."

Thony rolled his eyes. "Like anything *he* ever does is by accident. He said the 'Metreed' take care of Evil Wizards in the west," he told Dae.

Now her eyes went wide for real. "The *Metreedis?* Oh, wow," she said thoughtfully. "That would explain... so many things..."

"Like what?" Thony asked, distracted rather happily from the topic at hand, Dae thought.

"Oh, like how there isn't much call for mercenaries out that way," she explained. "We were all told not even to bother seeking our fortunes in that direction. The Metreedis control everything around the Merutian Sea," she explained. "At least until you get pretty far inland. And there's, oh, marshes and mountains and stuff. It's really so much harder to move around, even if some of those petty kingdoms have work for you. Nothing past the Misty Mountains is really worth it."

Thony was frowning. "The *'Merutian Sea',*" he muttered. "And *'Misty Mountains.'* Far to the west, lots of kingdoms... Damn, but I need a map."

Where *did* this boy come from, Dae wondered again, to have ended up a unicorn-maiden *and* not have ever heard of the Misty Mountains or the Merutian Sea... or the Metreedis. Maybe he really *had* been born on a farm, like that Jost-kid had suggested. But then why was he so worried about the Fairy Wood?

And... how had he met the Lost Princess of Pathremir and the King of the Pranksters?

Amanita was giving her a suspicious look.

There was another mystery. Amanita was clearly close friends with Thony, but for some reason she didn't seem to want him to know who she was.

"You were looking really thoughtful right there after we finished listening to the spies, Dae," Amanita noted carefully. "Was there something else you noticed?"

Dae was drawn back to the idea that had started fluttering around the back of her mind while she eavesdropped.

"Yes," she agreed. "Or, well, maybe. I keep thinking that I've heard their names before. Somewhere. Istevan and Shalladra, anyways. *Everyone* knows about Julanna Silversea."

And... oooh, wasn't *this* interesting? *Amanita* was giving her a confused look. And she wasn't bothering to hide *that* from Thony.

"Julanna Silversea?" Dae said remindingly. "You know, just about the most famous Bard ever to come out of the school in Selavan – and that's saying something. The song she graduated with pretty much forced King Mithral to make peace with the Disciples of the Goddess of Light. He actually married the Goddess of Light-and-Darkness' Chosen Disciple. And then he took on the demon that was haunting the Plains of Gavenor. With her at his side. His new queen, the Disciple, I mean, not

Julanna Silversea. Although I suppose they called on the God of Light and the Goddess of Light-and-Darkness to help them. A demon and all... what?"

The look on Amanita's face suggested that if she weren't already sitting down, she'd have done so – rather abruptly.

"They... *what?*"

"There's peace-talks going on between Dawil and Pathremir, too," Dae added helpfully, watching for the next reaction.

That apparently didn't faze the other girl. "I knew about *that,*" she said disapprovingly.

So. She had apparently been aware of what was going on for some time after she officially Disappeared. All the stuff in Selavan had happened in the last year or so.

But now Thony was looking at Amanita. "Does this change anything right now? Like, *tonight?*" he added with a strange emphasis.

Amanita shook herself slightly. "No... no. All of that other stuff... it should just make it easier to go home if we don't have to go by way of Sethival." She made a face. "No one in their right mind goes through Sethival. For anything. Trust me, I know."

Well, that explained what direction she'd gone when she left home, Dae thought.

This looked like it made no sense to Thony, but he nodded and yawned and stretched rather exaggeratedly. "I think I've had enough excitement for one evening. I'm going to bed."

"Good idea," Amanita added hastily. "I guess... we'll see you in the morning, Dae?"

"Not too early," Dae told them. "I probably should check in with the local Guild-house. It's something we're supposed to do right away when we get to a new place. So... maybe lunch?"

Their looks of relief convinced her that the two of them wouldn't be up before noon – likely sleeping off a late-night escapade. That they weren't planning on inviting her to join. And that they thought they had thrown her off the scent of trouble.

Yeah, right.

Even if Dae's nose for such things weren't her cutest and best feature, she was hardly going to let this pair out of her sight. Even if all she did was trail Amanita around – since the Lost Princess *did* seem to be planning to return to Pathremir – the Queen was likely to reward the mercenary who had guarded her only granddaughter successfully. And if Amanita changed her mind and Dae had to be a little more forceful to get her there – or at least go to Pathremir to tattle – then the reward was likely to be even *bigger*.

Dae's money troubles would be over, and likely her reputation salvag– erm, *made*.

And maybe it would even be enough to get Kamauri to quit trying to chase her down to 'make sure she was okay' and try to get her to go someplace safe.

Dae waved the others a cheery good-night and went out the door and then into her own room. There were preparations of her own that she'd like to make after all.

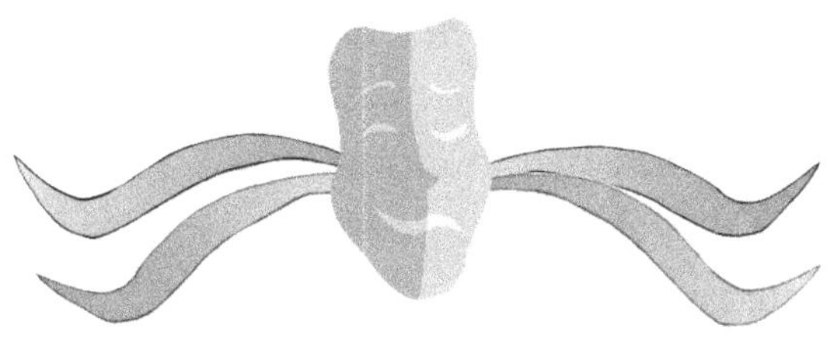

Chapter SIX

In the Middle of the Night

GETTING UP ONTO THE ROOF of the former-mayor's-mansion/Raven-troop-HQ was easier than figuring out how to get *inside* of it, Thony and Amanita discovered.

They were of one accord that they needed – possibly even more than Julanna and Istevan – to find out what Valderon Raven'sWing's plans were. And they were even of one accord about how to accomplish that goal.

Not like Istevan *(eeewww...)*, but by some good old-fashioned sneaking around.

They'd started out by going up on the roof of the inn – out of their window – to scout the lay of the land, as it were.

Thony – whose entire experience of buildings consisted of the Devinthals' castle and the entirely separate cottages in the nearby villages – was amazed to discover that the townsfolk had built their homes so close together that most of the roofs either touched or were close enough for a short leap to close the distance. The mountain-bred boy remembered that Flowerdust had stood up from the surrounding flat grasslands like a sore thumb, and was even more baffled. In Aldyrwald people built their homes in the valleys or wherever the ground was level enough to bother. Whyever did these plans-dwellers pack theirs so tightly when there was so much flat, buildable *space?*

Amanita tried explaining it as banding together for protection from thieves and bandits. But these rooftops practically formed a road – which surely should make the work of thieves easier – and it looked like Flowerdust's problem was less an issue of bandits than of invaders.

Thony just shook his head at the foibles of city-folks.

He'd had a feeling they were being followed, but Amanita had scoffed at the idea. And, honestly? They could see in pretty much every direction from up here, so it seemed pretty unlikely.

The mayoral mansion had a bit of a gap around it and then a wall, but the wall was full of chinks that made good toe- and finger-holds. And it was only a bit over six feet high, anyways. Thony could actually *reach* the top of it. And one of the sections of surrounding wall connected with an interior garden-wall, which connected to the roof of the mansion.

Clearly these people needed to rethink their architecture.

Or so he'd thought until they had discovered that there was no easy path *in* from the roof.

"This... may not have been the brightest idea," Amanita admitted after they had explored all the various gables.

Thony sighed. "I'm not sure there was a better one, though. I doubt the doors on the ground level are unlocked and unguarded both. Maybe when the mayor lived here–" they grinned at each other, having formed a similar opinion of the 'defenses,' "–but not with a professional paranoiac like Captain Shalladra in charge. I suppose we could try in the daytime," he suggested dubiously. "Come in as delivery people or messengers or something."

"If you're going to do that, you should go for cleaning staff," Dae informed them. "Cleaning staff can get in almost everywhere and people don't check them nearly as often as you might expect."

Thony just about had a heart attack – and it looked like Amanita was seriously considering one.

"What are *you* doing here?" the ex-stablegirl demanded.

"Following you," Dae replied jauntily. "And isn't it a good thing I did."

It wasn't really a question, the way she said it, but Amanita began to try to argue anyways.

She stopped, as Dae began to lay out some of the equipment she'd brought with her.

"That's a thief's lantern," Amanita accused her.

The lockpicking gear, rope, and a few other sundries was more what had caught Thony's eye than the rather normal-seeming lantern, but he quickly saw what Amanita meant. The thing was practically smokeless, shielded from all directions but one, and that last beam of light had a shield that could be quickly closed as well.

Dae shrugged. "Required for my Advanced Sneaking class at Sonoro's."

"You had a *class* on 'Advanced Sneaking'?" Thony asked enviously.

Maybe he could ditch this 'find a princess' jazz and go study to be a mercenary.

No, no, that would be irresponsible, Aldyrwald was depending on him, *yadda, yadda, yadda.*

Hmmmn... He had a few years to kill *(ha-ha)* before he could really go home and get married anyways. Maybe he could go enroll in this school and *then* go find his princess...

"Well, *they* called it 'Basic Camouflage'," Dae was saying. "But I mean what we were doing *was* sneaking. And I was already pretty good at that, but I got even better. I mean, you guys never even noticed I was following you."

Amanita was... trying to look skeptical and not impressed. "So, you never took 'Advanced Camouflage'?"

Dae shrugged. "Nah. I mean, I *did,* but it was all boring stuff. Like how to use magick to properly hide armies while they're advancing and all. I'm good at tactics, but strategy is *so* totally not my thing."

Amanita drew breath to respond to that, but Thony stepped close and put his hand over her mouth.

"So, you think you can get us into the mansion?" he asked.

"Sure." Dae shrugged again. "No biggie." She brandished a lockpick. "Let my enemies beware!"

"Ooww!" Thony yelped as Amanita bit his palm. They glared at each other for a moment.

"Thony's pretty good at picking locks," the ex-stablegirl commented. "I don't know that we need you for that."

Dae smirked at her. "But I know how to get inside the building."

Thony watched Amanita grind her teeth for a minute, then sighed. "Go ahead, Dae. Looks like we should have asked you to come along in the first place. I'll remember that for next time."

The mercenette looked pleased. "And so you should," she said, but before Amanita could take further umbrage, Dae led off across the roof.

Their entry point was a small window hidden under an eave where three different gables came together. It hadn't looked like there was enough space for even a person as small as Amanita to get in the space between the edges of the overhanging gables, so she and Thony had missed it on their own exploration of the roof. Dae admitted that she'd found the window by slipping and sliding down between the two overhangs. Thony took one look at the four-story drop from the bit of roof where she must have slid and shuddered.

Another thing to pin on the idiots who designed the buildings in this town. Why in the world did anyone here need a house that was four stories high?

The window let them into what should probably be an attic, based on location, but instead seemed – by the light of Dae's little thief's lantern – to be a sewing room that had recently been re-purposed as a weapons-care center. Given the sharply slanting ceilings, it hardly seemed suited to either activity.

For the tricksy trio's intents, however, it was perfect, since it was empty of people and appeared likely to stay that way for the duration of the night.

They opened the door cautiously and discovered that they were in the middle of a long hallway. A lantern glowed from around a corner at one end, giving them some faint light. Dae shuttered her thief's lantern.

With a few whispers and a lot of fairly useless hand-gestures, they split up – Dae went to the right, Amanita and Thony went to the left. The latter pair also split up when they reached the T-intersection at the end of the corridor. Amanita went to the left this time and Thony to the right, towards the lantern that he could now see hanging a dozen feet away.

The young prince made his way carefully along the dimly lit corridor, listening at each door for a moment as he went. Either the people withing were extremely quiet sleepers or the rooms were empty. Honestly, it didn't surprise him a great deal. Who would willingly make the fourth floor their quarters?

On the other hand, who would plan on having the fourth floor serve as a work-area? Wouldn't it make more sense to stash the people up here and have the areas they were coming and going from be more accessible?

Or maybe there weren't that many Raven troops in Flowerdust after all. Thony had seen them patrolling when he was walking around with Amanita earlier, but never more than four and an officer at a time. And while the people – as Amanita had noted the previous night – *looked* fearful and the innkeeper had practically stuttered in his attempt to serve Captain Shalladra... they didn't appear particularly *downtrodden*.

At least not *yet*. Or maybe that was '*at least not the way Thony imagined*' that '*downtrodden*' should look. He'd never seen that before either, after all, any more than he'd been able to identify the people drinking at the Inn of the Starred Hoof as '*looking fearful*' the way Amanita had. He was taking her word on that.

Which made him wonder if he really wanted to follow her back to her homeland. Where had she learned to identify *fear* in people's faces, anyways?

Something else to try to eke out of her.

At least the one thing they had settled, while Dae had picked the lock on the window, was a more specific purpose for this mission: they were to look for any evidence of what this war was about and what the Evil Wizard's plans were. And they would wreak what havoc they could along the way – since, well, that was about what a bunch of kids really could *do* against an invading army.

Dae, it turned out, *was* a prankster as well, and was onboard with the plan as soon as Amanita had suggested it. Given her accident-prone nature, Thony was just as pleased that she was investigating the headquarters house in the opposite direction as himself. They wanted to make it look like the *Raven-troops* were having a run of bad luck – to mess with their morale, at least – not get themselves caught and flayed alive or whatever that creepy Captain Shalladra might think up to do with them.

There was a stairwell at the end of the young prince's corridor. It led down, with exits on each floor. The stairwell itself had a threadbare carpet on the steps, no banister, and was fairly narrow. A servants' accessway, he suspected. Which might suggest that those fourth-story rooms were the ones where the servants *normally* resided.

Where they were now, he couldn't guess – surely the Raven troops and their commander needed domestic duties done as much as the former mayor and his family had. Or were they so paranoid that they'd fired all the staff?

Thony passed all the various doors, going down a full four flights of stairs, which put him a level below ground-level. To his not-terribly-great surprise, he found himself at the domestic facilities for the building.

Which were clearly still in heavy use, although at this late hour they were far emptier than the Royal Kitchens ever were back home. No cooks or maids finding a warm spot to sleep beside the banked fire in the large hearth. No sleepy manservant minding a pot of stew or tea or ready to leap to answer the bell-pull of the lord or lady of the house.

Not even a kitchen cat skulking around to keep mice down.

Not even a mouse skittering away as Thony skulked around.

There *were* a series of bowls with damp cloths covering them set out on a table that wasn't too far from the fire. So, at least someone had left bread to rise overnight if they did food here the way it worked at home. The dough was shielded from the direct heat of the fire, presumably to slow the rise until the cooks returned to start the morning baking.

Thony had a certain familiarity with rising dough *(long story)* but it wasn't easy to look at the bowls and figure out how much longer they were expected to rise. Hours, at least, was his guess, but was more because of the level of paranoia that seemed to have resulted in the nighttime dismissal of the staff than by any familiarity with bread. If you wanted breakfast on time, but didn't want cooks to stay in the kitchen, you had better let them in early... but not *too* early...

Without clocks – and neither Amanita nor Dae had mentioned clocks or how long a day was – he had to guess it was a bit after midnight, but not a very great *deal* past midnight. And that he had a fair bit of time before the cooks returned.

Thony looked around himself with appreciation. In a place like this – and with no one to get in his way and no real practical limitations on his creativity for kindness' sake – the possibilities were *endless*.

The runaway prince grinned to himself and set to work.

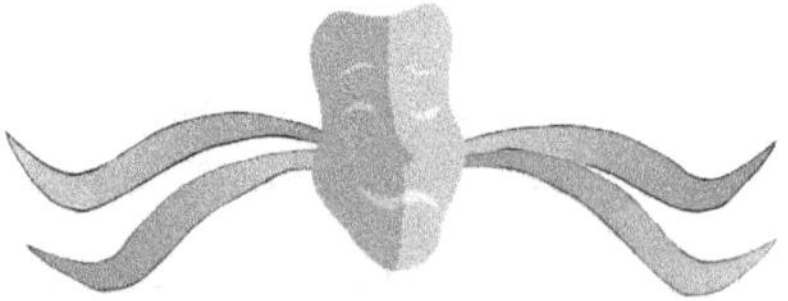

Dae Goldeneyes slunk ostentatiously down the corridor for a good long while, even going down a staircase a level, reveling in the joy of using some of her favorite skills. Though her sneaking *was* a little rusty, if she wanted to be honest about it.

Honestly, being a Royal Bodyguard for a kid who was far too good for his own good had been Super Boring. You'd think that knowing he was the Heir to the Throne and all would have given Harper a sense of invincibility that he would have wanted to test out... and that having a bodyguard who was practically his own age and Totally Willing to get into trouble and take all the blame would have upped his sense of adventure. But, no.

She'd been about ready to absolutely Die of Boredom *(even if they were paying her decently)* when the whole incident with the duchess' gown had occurred. Which had definitely livened things up.

Dae would never admit to relief at getting fired... let alone at there being a rather *not-accidental* component to the whole thing.

Staying in one place for years and years and *years,* and standing around *waiting for something to happen* was totally not her style.

Sneaking around the headquarters of an invading army and rescuing a Lost Princess totally *was.*

Things were certainly looking up in Dae's world.

Now, if only she could get whomever was in charge over at the Flowerdust Mercenaries' Guildhouse to tell Kamauri *(whenever she showed up)* that Dac had been and gone... and if Kamauri would just *believe* that and then go on to wherever Dae left word she 'was heading'... Maybe the mercenette wouldn't have to stay on the run.

It was darned hard to find a decent job when you were fourteen, looked two years younger than that, and had to keep fleeing from your best friend. But Kamauri refused to believe Dae was capable of taking care of herself, despite the fact that she'd been *doing so* for the last two years.

Maybe with a few mishaps along the way, but nobody had *died.*

Dae pulled her mind back to the job at hand.

First-class sneaking and mischief-making required attention.

And... it occurred to her that:

1) it wasn't likely she could actually *make* any mischief if she didn't actually enter any of these rooms she was sneaking past; and

2) how was she supposed to find her way back to the sewing room-cum-weapons-repair facility since she hadn't been paying attention to which way she'd been going and there had been a few turns and branches?

Number Two would come out all right on its own, she assumed. It usually did, after all, so long as one had a few prunes handy.

Number One she could begin on right now.

Stealthily, she edged up to the next door on her left, listening carefully at the crack and even holding her breath for a few seconds to be sure all was silent. She was good at sneaking around sleeping people *(it was how she'd gotten past Kamauri every time her friend had caught up with her, after all... and, um, out of that dungeon that her former employer had put her in for a little while)*, but it was good to know what one was getting into before one got into it. When possible, anyways, not that *not* knowing had ever stopped her.

Carefully, she eased the door open...

... and was met with a rather more complete blackness than she had expected from a second-story room. Not even a hint of light from a window – and there was both a full moon out and torches burning in most of the courtyards around the mansion, so there should have been *something*.

Cursing silently about how much easier this would all have been in the daytime *(ignoring little issues regarding logistics and secrecy, but those sorts of things never bothered Dae),* she unshielded her tiny thief's lantern...

... to find herself looking into a linen-closet.

After all that fuss, a *linen-closet.* Or really, more of a linen-*pantry,* since it was more like a small room with rows of shelves neatly stacked with sheets and pillowcases and blankets and quilts and towels. A bin at the far end was empty, but clearly meant for retrieval of dirties so they could be taken down to the laundry.

With a disappointed sigh, Dae re-shielded her lantern and silently closed the door.

There were other rooms, after all.

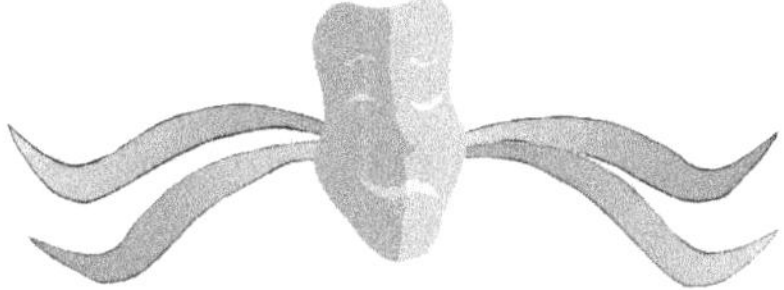

The last of the intended troublemakers, Amanita was proceeding much as Dae had, though with perhaps a little more focus.

She had gone down *two* levels when she found the house's grand staircase, guessing that the fancier rooms would be there. The original owner of the mansion surely wouldn't have wanted to have to traipse up and down extra stairs, if things were done here the way Amanita had seen elsewhere. Including at home.

Her guesses seemed good, and she was able to slip into several rooms to confirm that there was silver braid on the sleeves of the uniform jackets hung up on hooks or laid over the backs of chairs. Not all the rooms were occupied by their owners *(or their owners' clothing),* but even those had signs that they weren't inhabited by common riff-raff.

She took note of what was in each room. There was nothing terribly handy for making mischief on – well, nothing *subtle,* and she didn't want to resort to such crudities as tipping over inkwells. Such things would make it all too obvious that someone else had been there, which wouldn't work well with the idea of there being a simple run of bad luck.

However, with the proper preparation, the proper tools... there was a great deal she could do on their *next* venture into this mansion.

Amanita was saving the master suite for last, figuring that she'd spend the remainder of her time there.

It was... even more massive than she'd expected, and ridiculously luxurious for the mayor of such a small town in the middle of nowhere as Flowerdust. Apparently, the mayor had *pretensions,* as her father's mother would have put it. Eldest-Princess Reyalla had little patience with commoners getting above themselves.

The suite seemed to consist of four rooms. Each was lit by a small lantern, presumably so that the Captain didn't have to risk barking her shins no matter what time she came in. It was an extravagance, given the prices for lamp-oil that Amanita had noted passingly in the market, but it was handy for her, so she was hardly going to complain.

The other officers' quarters had been entirely dark, and she *had* suffered some barked shins, that were still annoying her, due to some chairs that seriously did *not* belong where they'd been left. At least that had only been in the empty rooms, so her muffled *yelp* hadn't been marked. It had taken some self-control not to begin reorganizing those rooms immediately.

Each of the four rooms also seemed to be connected to all the others, as well as to external passages, so there were an unreasonable number of doors. The girl couldn't decide if this suggested that the owner was incredibly trusting or incredibly paranoid.

Or maybe it was simply a matter of convenience, since some of those extra doors probably opened onto servants' hallways so that the suite could be serviced without *(gasp)* having the servants use the more majestic public entrances.

First, was an office that was clearly designed to intimidate. The desk was massive, though it was only made of polished maple – though Amanita supposed that even maple was probably fairly dear out here on the plains. The chairs facing it were hard and slightly lower than most chairs, while the richly upholstered one behind the desk was slightly higher and with a footrest – so visitors would be at an immediate disadvantage.

The walls were tastefully lined with tapestries and paintings and bookshelves. It was impossible, in this light, to determine the subject-matter of the art, but Amanita was able to peek behind them to determine that all that was there was more wall. No hidden doors or cabinets.

The bookshelves were even more disappointing. The 'books' were apparently all for show. Despite the titles etched on the spines in gold leaf, they were simply leatherbound boxes. Clearly the former mayor's *pretensions* extended to making others think of her as erudite and educated without any factual basis.

The desk drawers were all empty – and dust-filled, which made her wrinkle her nose and her fingers twitch for dusting cloths. One of the things she had enjoyed most in Aldyrwald was the chance to actually clean things to her own satisfaction. At home... well, *that* wasn't going to happen. Her own rooms had been impeccable, of course, but the rest of the palace...

Next to the show-office was a sitting room that was also arranged with a sort of stilted elegance. It was possible to imagine snooty-looking people having tea here and trying to one-up each other... but not so much someone curled up on the overstuffed sofa to read one of the non-existent books from the office.

The third room – central to the rest and accessible to all of them – was an overly elaborate washroom. Amanita took the opportunity to wash her hands after checking the cleanliness of the handtowels.

The final room was, of course, a bedroom. It featured an enormous four-poster bed with a canopy and curtains, as if it were made for royalty. A huge wardrobe took up most of one wall and a vanity with a huge mirror had pride-of place on the opposite wall. A small, utilitarian-looking desk squatted next to the wardrobe in the back corner beside the bed, its square construction at odds with the graceful curves of the rest of the furniture. A door that didn't lead back to sitting-room or office or bath probably let onto the servants' passageways, but it was locked.

The girl gravitated to the desk and the neat stacks of papers arranged around its surface.

A great *many* stacks of papers: some of them had been migrated to the floor, though they were stacked with military precision. Amanita rather approved of that, although when she crouched down to examine them, she got a peek under the bed and saw dust-bunnies the size of *hamsters*...

She kind of wished she had a thief's lantern now herself, but the lamp that was already alight in this room was set on the desk anyways, so it wasn't too bad. She didn't quite dare turn up the light, but it was enough to see by.

Likely these were the papers that Lieutenant Istevan had put so much, erm, *effort* into getting access to. So, he'd probably been through all of them.

On the other hand, he and his fellow conspirators seemed to know a lot more about what was going on than Amanita did.

She hadn't missed that Dae was testing her with that little update about Selavan.

Not that she was sure she believed that story. The *Líonar* people had fled out of Pathremir in that direction, too, when Pathremir had been liberated. The Selavani were their descendants as well, and therefore not to be trusted any more than the ones to the west, in Mountainmeadow. It was bad enough that trade had to go one way or the other.

In any case, Amanita simply didn't know what was going on with Valderon Raven'sWing and this little war of his well enough to know what they needed to look for. *Anything* she found would be helpful to her and her friends, even stuff that might simply be dismissed by Istevan and his crew.

If only Puck had been willing to give them a few more details...

Or if Dae didn't seem too scatterbrained to understand the strategic situation... the girl had basically admitted that she simply didn't *care* about such things.

Which... maybe made a certain amount of sense. After all, as a mercenary, Dae probably had *more* job opportunities if there was a war on. Even if she didn't want to join in a full-blown battlefield – and, realistically, that probably wasn't a good option for someone her size – there were probably way more people wanting guards to protect them from the conflict.

Amanita found a number of things that fit the category of '*Istevan probably wouldn't care but we would*' almost immediately, as she examined the papers.

There was a map, for instance, that was color-coded. And had arrows on it and numbers. It bore more detailed examination than she could fairly give it under the circumstances, so she rolled it up to take with her. Given that the desk was so well-organized and the map was under three other stacks – and was with a handful of unmarked maps – it didn't look like it was something Shalladra would be needing immediately.

Amanita took one of the unmarked maps also. She'd transfer all the information and bring back the original in a day or two.

But while she was carefully shifting piles of papers around, she noticed a set that was placed so that they wouldn't be noticed by a less determined searcher. Awkward to get to and more than half-hidden... but tied in two directions with what might be a red ribbon. And a bow.

Love-letters?

Did even the icicle-hearted Captain Shalladra have someone she cared about? Or... was she evil enough herself to lovingly tie up detailed descriptions of torture methods or something?

With a certain morbid curiosity, Amanita picked up the packet and brought it into the lamp-light, determined to return it to its hiding place as soon as she was sure it was just weirdly gooey girly stuff. She didn't really *want* to see the Captain as having human emotions, but...

Her intent to put the packet back vanished when she realized that the signature scrawled with a dramatic flourish across the top page was that of Valderon Raven'sWing.

Amanita had hit paydirt.

Unfortunately, there were also noises coming from the direction of the show-office.

It didn't sound like there was time to dash across to the door into the sitting-room or washroom – and by the voices, it was Captain Shalladra and she wasn't alone. A man's voice – probably Istevan, which meant this had taken longer than Amanita thought...

She quickly considered and discarded the idea of hiding under the bed. Trapped under there with the dust-bunnies... no.

Instead, she hurried into the gigantic wardrobe, hoping that there would be no reason for anyone to look in there...

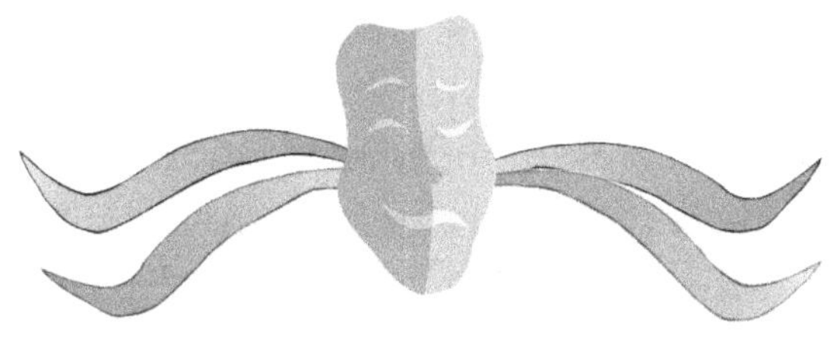

Chapter SEVEN

Enlightenment Dawns

THONY RETURNED TO THE SEWING room-cum-weapons-care center where they had snuck in to find Dae had beat him there. She was sitting in the light of her tiny thief's lantern and seemed to be paring her fingernails with a gigantic knife.

"How did it go?" he asked when she seemed to be between fingers.

The mercenette gave a nonchalant shrug that was rather spoiled by her smug grin. "Oh, you know. I spilled a few inkwells, soaked all the towels, tied some bootlaces together, switched some clothes around between different trunks and such. That sort of thing."

"So, you found the barracks then?" Thony asked.

"Yep," Dae agreed cheerily. "How about you?"

"I ended up in the kitchens and laundry," the young prince said. "Lots of opportunities there."

He had started out with a barrel of apples. First, he had painstakingly drilled holes in a handful of apples, and then trimmed narrow strips of uncooked roast. The ribbons of rubbery, pink meat had been carefully stuffed into the holes in the apples and the apples themselves mixed back into the top few layers in the barrel. Whomever cut – or bit – into the apples should think there were worms.

Thony had then gone on to break off bits of bread from the previous day's baking to make it look like the loaves had been nibbled by mice. The effect was somewhat marred by the fact that he couldn't – on the spur of the moment – come up with anything to resemble mouse-droppings to spread around. Mice never ate anything without leaving abundant poopy evidence of their presence *(which had been the part of his rat-training program that had been the most work to deal with)*, but perhaps it would be overlooked.

In the mansion's laundry room, the victims of his attack had been the socks and hose waiting to be cleaned. It had been smelly work *(didn't these people ever wash their feet?)*, but Thony had been willing to endure for the Greater Good. *(Notwithstanding the clothespin he put on his nose.)*

Some of the stockings and hosiery he simply tied together, some he stuffed inside each other, and some he hid in a basket of cleaned, folded laundry where it wouldn't be easily found. *(He still wondered if he'd gone over the line with that last.)*

The young prince was absolutely *dying* for Dae to ask him for the details so he could regale her... but, alas, she merely nodded and went back to what she had been doing.

Dear Gods. Was that a *hunting* knife she was using on her nails? Surely it was too big for safety...

...and now she was pulling off her left boot, apparently to begin work on her toes.

Thony looked back at the door, wondering how much longer Amanita would be. Longer than this, it seemed.

He settled himself down to watch Dae's efforts at not accidentally amputating anything with a sort of morbid curiosity and wait for his missing friend.

... and wait... and wait... and wait...

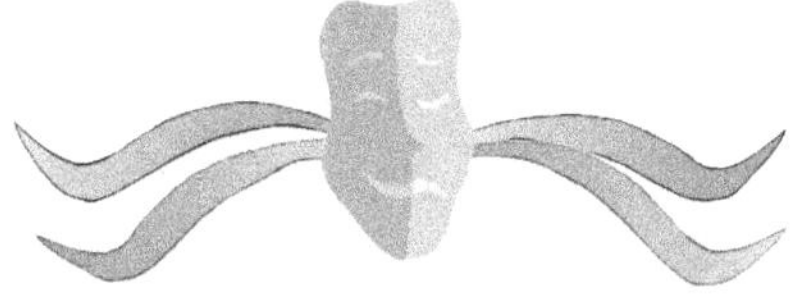

The sky was perceptibly lighter by the time Amanita finally showed up.

The other two arose immediately, Dae taking time to pull on her boot first. Thony gestured them urgently to the window.

By unspoken agreement they put off conversation until they had made it to a rooftop several streets away. The sky was *distinctly* lighter now, and Thony would have sworn he could see the first rays of sunlight from this height. He reminded himself that sunrise on this flat land meant something different in terms of time than sunrise in a mountain-valley like Aldyrwald. There weren't even cows lowing yet to be milked... though, come to think of it, he hadn't seen any cows in the town.

That seemed odd. Every villager in Aldyrwald had a milch-beast and a coop of chickens or ducks or geese out behind their cottage to supply the family's needs. The farmer with the dairy-herd supplied the castle with butter and milk and cheese, and a handful of goodwives kept extra fowl to supply the castle's needs for eggs and poultry. Half the cottages bought a piglet from the farmer who kept sows as well, though he and the cowherd with the beef cattle had a monopoly on the castle's meat – save for when Papa's knights and huntsmen went out for venison or boar or pheasant. Rabbit wasn't to be found on the royal table, of course, but the village-boys trapped the wild ones and kept other ones that the Springtime Bunny brought each year in hutches until they were ready for the table.

The town suddenly seemed weirdly silent to the young prince without the usual clatter of cows and crowing cocks and snorting pigs that had been audible even up at the castle.

Where did the people of Flowerdust even get their eggs and milk? He'd seen all the fruits and vegetables for sale in the market the previous day, but had been too boggled by the size of the town to much mark exactly what was being sold. Besides, Amanita had mentioned that it was early Spring here *(despite it being close to Midsummer at home)* and people always needed to buy from the farmers' Winter stores come Spring...

He shook off the minor mystery and focused on the two girls, who seemed to be facing off and glaring at each other.

"Well, *you* sure took your own sweet time," Dae commented with more sharpness than he had heard from the mercenette before. Thony had sort of begun to assume that she was permanently set on 'happy-go-lucky.'

"Well, *excuuuuuse* me," Amanita snapped back.

"There's no excuse for you!" Dae retorted, but the twinkle had returned to her eyes.

Amanita set her fists on her hips.

Thony sighed internally. Clearly, he was going to have to break this up.

He stepped between the two girls and placed a hand in front of each of their chests *(carefully not making contact – because that would be **weird**)* and said "Alright now. Break it up. *Break it up.*"

They stared at him disbelievingly for a moment, then looked at each other, then stared at him again, then finally nodded knowingly at each other. It was a move clearly calculated to drive Thony *nuts.*

And it worked.

"Will you two cut it out?" he said peevishly. "I want to know what took you so long, 'Nita, and go back to the inn. It's been a long night and I need my beauty sleep."

He realized what he'd handed them wrapped in gilt and paper and with a big bow *almost* before their grins widened wickedly.

"You two could do with some of that yourselves," he added hastily, trying to look critical instead of exhausted and not to say it too fast.

"Humph." Amanita said.

"So how was *your* night, 'Nita'?" Dae asked brightly.

Was it Thony's imagination that he could hear quotation marks around Amanita's nickname? He tried to think back and remember if he'd slipped up and called his friend by her full-name instead of the alias she'd been insisting on. If he had, she was going to be so... *irritated*. Especially if it meant Dae had figured out who she really was.

Heck, if *Dae* – whom they'd known for less than a full *(ahem)* day knew who his best friend was better than he did... *Thony* was going to be pretty darn *irritated* himself!

"Pretty useful, actually," Amanita began. "Even though I didn't get to play any pranks–"

"Poor 'Nita'," Dae grinned without a trace of sympathy. "Didn't get *any* fun."

"Well...." Amanita considered the comment. "Actually, that's true," she conceded, "but it certainly wasn't Dullsville. In fact–"

And she proceeded to give them a rather hair-raising account of her nighttime adventures.

Thony listened with a mix of awe and envy as she described hiding in the wardrobe as Captain Shalladra and Lieutenant Istevan came in. There had apparently been a knothole in the wood of the wardrobe door that let her peer out.

Istevan, she reported, had looked disheartened and exhausted. Shalladra had made some rather genteel-sounding threats and... well, Amanita had covered her ears and tried to ignore what went on after that. She'd managed to sneak out eventually when Istevan got up to pace and Shalladra sleepily ordered him out because he was disturbing her rest. He hadn't noticed the small girl slipping out behind him when he exited into the office.

He'd made it out onto the one-sided corridor that overlooked the main entry hall before Amanita had managed to catch up with him. She'd heard his boots thumping down the elegant main stairs, but he'd been out of sight before she'd managed to ease the main door to the suite closed silently – she had no idea if Captain Shalladra was a light enough sleeper to notice that the outer door had closed twice; it had been all Amanita could do to manage the inner door when she'd followed Istevan out of the bedroom.

She'd wasted some time trying to figure out where he'd gone, then come back to meet up with the others.

"So, let's see these papers you found," Dae said rather prosaically as Amanita finished her tale with a flourish.

The ex-stablegirl looked a bit put out, but reached inside her tunic to extract them. They all sat down on the rooftop as she spread out the map, setting the tied bundle to one side. The sky was bright enough now to examine her treasures without needing the thief's lantern.

Thony found himself looking at the first map of the region that he'd seen and was torn between trying to memorize all the strange place-names and geography... and between being horrified by how much territory was covered with blue shading to indicate that it was controlled by Valderon Raven'sWing. As Amanita had noticed earlier, there were also numbers and arrows and other notations.

"There were several unmarked maps with this one," the girl said. "I grabbed one of those, too. I'll need to stop in the market tomorrow – er, today – to pick up ink or pencils, but I want to transfer all the marks to the blank and then sneak this original back in."

"I have ink and a pen," Thony said absently, one finger tracing the arrows on the map. "These numbers can't be right, can they?"

Amanita peered down. "Why?"

"Aren't they rather, well, *small?*"

Dae leaned in, curiously. "Oh, that's mercenary shorthand for battle-units. You know, squads, platoons, that sort of thing. The numbers inside each symbol refer to how many are at that location. These," she pointed to one type of mark, "indicate platoons – that's twenty people plus an officer, usually. And these are for companies of one hundred. There are between three and five officers with each of those. And these are battalions..." Her voice trailed off.

After a moment, Thony cleared his throat. "How many in a battalion?"

The mercenette bit her lip. "It... varies. Some countries – like the one where I was a bodyguard – call three companies put together under one commander a battalion."

"And others?" Thony asked. It couldn't be good news, not if she was dragging it out like this.

"A thousand soldiers," Dae said quietly.

Thony blinked. The symbols she had pointed out had *numbers* inside them... small, single digit numbers, but still. And there were *more than one* of those, in addition to the other symbols.

"That can't be right," Amanita said with a frown. "Dawil is the richest country I know and this is almost more people than they have under arms. And *they* can't field this many people all in one place. It takes a *lot* of farmers and tradeswomen to support *one* soldier or knight."

Dae looked up at her. "We studied Dawil in class. They have three hostile powers on their borders as well as all that coastline and their shipping to defend from pirates. If they *could* put all their military in one place, they'd be close to unstoppable, but then they'd lose their other fronts."

Amanita frowned harder. "Well, Selavan and Sethival then. They don't have above five thousand people under arms. Sethival might have seven," she said grudgingly. "If King Tameran drafts in all the fighters under his marcher barons at once. But *they* couldn't put them all in the field either." She swallowed hard. "Pathremir... doesn't have *half* that many."

It seemed... odd that Amanita just had all these *other* numbers ready to hand to pull out and compare.

Thony was still trying to wrap his head around the numbers at all. Warfare, in the Mountain Region that Aldyrwald was a part of, counted armies in the scores or even a few hundreds. Not since historical times had there been a battle involving a thousand men – and that would have been counting both sides at once.

It took close to ten peasants to support one man under arms. There were plenty of knights – but they engaged in duels of honor or defended the roads against marauding bandits and ogres and dragons, all the while hoping that they would win a princess – or at least a noble heiress. Outfitting and maintaining a knight was either his own lookout – paid for by intimidating local villagers and at risk of being chased off by the local king's own knights – or was taken care of by the king he was sworn to. There wasn't enough money to keep more than a handful of peasants under arms as castle guardsmen and such, and even they usually had to be given time off for planting and harvest.

That was why wars in the Mountain Region had to be restricted to the hottest part of Summer, when the crops more or less took care of themselves, or else after the harvest was in. Summer warfare was hindered by the fields – trampling the crops risked a famine for the entire region – and Winter warfare was rendered close to impossible by the heavy snowfalls that were typical. But those were the only time the peasants were available to...

Suddenly it occurred to him what they were missing.

Well, he and Amanita, anyways. Dae seemed to be trying not to say it out loud – because it would make the other two look bad? Or because she didn't want to be the bearer of bad news?

"These aren't *standing armies*," Thony managed to say. "They're impressed troops. The places they're being taken from – there's no one left behind to... to run the farms and prepare for the Spring planting."

And care for the children and elderly, tend the gardens, weave the cloth, milk the cows – assuming the armies hadn't taken all the livestock, like Puck had mentioned when they arrived... Could women even *do* all those things on their own?

Or... and it was a worse thought yet... had even the women and older children been left behind? Shalladra was a woman and a soldier. So was Dae.

Secretly learning from Roger and Jeremy how to use a sword and a bow back at home had been fun and it had made the young prince feel like *somebody* at least took him seriously.

Mama and Papa didn't, after all, coddling Thony and preventing him even from roaming out of sight of the castle and not letting him learn any useful outdoorsy skills. Great-Uncle Sir Eddie, who was his riding instructor hadn't either.

And the squires and pages – and knights – certainly hadn't, for all that someday they'd be kneeling at Thony's feet to swear as his vassals. In their case, there had been a definite sense that a man who couldn't handle himself on a Quest – who couldn't use a sword and a bow and build a fire and all the rest – wasn't really a *man*.

Crown Prince or not.

King, or not.

So, Thony had *liked* learning the new skills, even if he hadn't been able to tell all of those other people that he was doing so. And he'd carefully put aside just why a man needed to learn how to handle a sword at all...

The idea of men – of *belted knights* – meeting upon the field of honor to do damage to each other was bothersome.

The thought of bringing dozens or hundreds *(Thony's mind quailed away from the word 'thousands')* of peasant men in for larger battles... The historical descriptions of the destruction and harms done in the Bad Old Days had been exactly what had caused him to swear his childhood oath to never let that happen again to Aldyrwald.

And... he'd known that women and children and old people were the ones who suffered a great many of those 'harms'... But he'd never, in his wildest, darkest imaginations put those women and children out on the battlefield *themselves*.

But Dae was nodding soberly. "Probably. Which means that all this territory – the sorcerer-dude hasn't *taken* that territory. He's conquered it, and possibly smashed it too badly for whomever is left to rebel... But he's not creating a new nation out here. He's... collecting troops for some other purpose."

"To conquer the rich countries to the west," Amanita looked horrified.

Thony was still worried that a man that could think on this large of a scale had even bigger plans than that. He'd found the legend on the map and calculated out the distances involved; the whole of the Mountain Region could *fit inside* the area that was shaded.

"Let's... take a look at those letters," he suggested, as much to distract them all from the horribleness of what they were looking at as out of actual curiosity.

They had to put these things back, after all, so they had better get a look as quickly as possible. His first reaction had been that while the map might be a problem, a stack of love-letters was probably both useless and irreplaceable.

But he'd noted Valderon Raven'sWing's signature when Amanita had flourished the packet in front of them.

Amanita nodded sharply and bent to carefully picking apart the ribbons tying up the packet. They'd have to re-tie it *exactly* when they returned it, after all.

Thony stood up to stretch and pace while she worked on it.

At last, the ribbons fell away and they all crowded around while the ex-stablegirl carefully lifted the topmost page and read aloud:

To Shalladra, Captain-Mayoress and Representative of Myself in Flowerdust:

This missive is to inform you that the preparations to march on the Fairy Wood are nearly complete, and the army should arrive in Flowerdust in three weeks. I may arrive somewhat sooner, conditions permitting.

The regular troops are still learning to manage the ones 'acquired' here in Darjil, but they have arrived at a fairly efficient mode of incentivizing them to move.

Upon my arrival, you will be relieved of your command in Flowerdust. Captain Fayorn will assume control of the town. A field-command awaits you – I want you at my side during the campaign to come, for I have no one more loyal than yourself.

Be sure that Flowerdust is prepared to meet any last provisioning needs for the army – a task which should be simple, based on the reports you have been sending me regarding the submissiveness of the population. I look forwards to seeing such a docile town after our recent efforts in Tarivor, Grains-of-Gold, and Cadrin.

I shall expect Flowerdust and its garrison to be ready for Captain Fayorn to assume command upon my arrival, and for you yourself to be prepared to take your proper place at my side. While I know that you appreciate the importance of this long and tedious assignment, and why you were the only person I could trust to secure this entry-point to the Wood, your military genius has been sorely missed while we have pursued the other goals in your absence.

By the hand of your King and Commander-General,

Valderon Raven'swing
Regis-Magicus

"It's dated... a week ago," Amanita finished, her voice trailing off. She raised her eyes to meet Thony's.

"So, you were right, Thony," Dae said, her own gaze still scanning the paper. "The Fairy Wood *is* his objective." She tugged at the letter to get a better look.

Amanita handed it to her. "It doesn't make *sense*," the ex-stablegirl complained, though there was a note of guilty relief in her voice. "Even if Puck doesn't reach Queen Lilysong in time, the Dark-elves and Light-elves are still there to protect the Wood. And if *they* should somehow fail, there're so many *other* things... just moving through the Wood at *all* should be impossible without expert guides."

Thony shivered at the thought of war descending on *Aldyrwald* from such a completely unexpected source. Or on Eyola, where Midele and Girona's people didn't sound capable of defending themselves. Not that Aldyrwald was set to defend against numbers like *these*...

"Or the Perushin village," Amanita agreed, "or – oh, tons of place we've never even heard of!"

He must have muttered some of that aloud, Thony realized.

Gods, but he wanted to go *home* and at least *warn* them.

But Queen Lilysong had said that travel through the Wood was closed to him and Amanita until they completed some task. And the Fairy Queen had refused to tell them what that task was. Which didn't help at *all*.

He felt an arm around his shoulders. The young prince hadn't even realized he'd fallen to his knees, but she was on one knee beside him. She couldn't have reached his shoulders like this if they were both standing, after all.

"It'll be okay, Thony," Amanita said gently. "Even if Raven'sWing manages to get himself and his troops into the Fairy Wood *and* get them to some other world – chances are it wouldn't be *yours*. Or Eyola," she added after a moment.

He looked at her with sudden hope. "Isn't it just as likely that they'll run into that lava-world you mentioned? Or the one with the carnivorous plants?"

Dae was looking them with a great deal of interest, but Thony wasn't up for trying to explain.

Amanita winced. "About those... I don't know if they're actually *real*. Quellarie – the person who told me about them – was trying to warn me off of traveling the Wood at all. I'm not sure if she might have... exaggerated."

That... wasn't an appealing thought. Well, except for the idea that it might make it easier to get home.

"And *we* didn't get lost even though we went off the established path..." Thony noted with dismay.

The ex-stablegirl shrugged, but she seemed to be looking at Dae. "I don't know. There is dangerous stuff. The *findilaar* that attacked us. *Glypherthryps*... I don't know what all else. But... I have to wonder how much of crossing safely is just knowing where you're trying to go."

Thony frowned. "But... Eyola... and you said you randomly ended up in the Perushin village while trying to reach *my* world...?"

Amanita shrugged uncomfortably. "I don't know. But in any case, I don't think *anyone* travels the Wood without Queen Lilysong's at least tacit approval. She *is* the Guardian of the Ways Between the Worlds, after all. As Puck told us, the Power of the Wood all emanates from Her originally."

"True..." Thony took a deep breath, though it still came in kind of stuttery, so he was clearly *not* yet okay with all of this...

"Actually..." Dae's voice was reluctant.

Thony looked up to meet her eyes.

The mercenette looked more serious – and more capable – than she had up until now. Far less the goofy ne'er-do-well and far more the trained professional... warrior.

"Actually what?" Amanita asked warily.

Dae focused on her. "*You* should know if anyone does, your – you're from Pathremir. Even Goddesses can be leveraged. Didn't the Silver Dragon abandon your people for a thousand years while they were being oppressed? Did She ever explain why?"

The ex-stablegirl's warmly reassuring arm around Thony was suddenly as cold as *he* felt. "Yes... When She came back to us, She told Queen Varella that She had other responsibilities."

Dae nodded, looking grim. "And your people were being *slaughtered,* weren't they?"

"Not... not exactly..." Amanita was shaking a little now, and Thony put an arm around *her.* The rooftop they were on wasn't very steeply slanted, but it wasn't a good place to be having these sorts of revelations if they were reacting like this.

On the other hand, he didn't really feel steady enough to maneuver across all the roofs left between them and the inn, and then clamber back down into the window of their room.

"What does 'not exactly slaughtered' mean?" he asked.

The girl's fists clenched. "My people were enslaved. By a handful of refugees from another world that we had welcomed with open arms."

Thony looked at her in horror. "Wait... 'refugees from another world'? Doesn't that mean Queen Lilysong *let* them come through? Why would She *do* that? And your *own* Goddess couldn't help you?"

Not that the Deities back home were terribly interventionist – before Roger and Joanna and Priscilla had become Gods,

Thony hadn't even been entirely sure that Gods were *real*. And even now it wasn't clear that Roger and Joanna and Priscilla would actually protect Aldyrwald if things fell out the way he and Papa feared. If They'd been able to be sure of that, Thony wouldn't have had to go on his Quest, after all.

The other Two – Phillip and Cythera – had said some things during the discussions after Roger and Joanna's second wedding, about how 'mortals must do for themselves.' Cythera was Goddess of Fire and Phillip was God of Water – and They came from another world *(this one? He wasn't sure)* so They had no real vested interest in the particular people living in Aldyrwald. But Roger and Thony's sisters had nodded and looked unhappy... and then Phillip had 'reminded' Them that They might have been *born* here but They were beholden to the whole world

Amanita nodded tightly. "We... still don't pray to the Great Goddess – the Waywalker. I actually didn't know that Queen Lilysong was one of Her Aspects until Puck mentioned it."

The expression on her face suggested that she'd been trying not to think about it since she'd found out. Amanita had *liked* the Fairy Queen, Thony recalled, and the feeling had seemed to be mutual.

Though there might be some question of whether you could ever really know what an immortal – even one that wasn't a God – was thinking.

Which set up an uncomfortable corollary to his own relationship with his sisters and Roger...

"And... this other Goddess," he asked awkwardly. "The Dragon one? You – or all of you – forgave Her?"

Amanita shrugged one shoulder. "There's all this stuff the priestesses tell us about how She *couldn't* help us because of those *other responsibilities*. Which had something to do with guarding us all from what else might be trying to come after the *Líonar* people. I don't know. And that She came back as soon as she could. My grandmother says it's all true, though, and *she* should know if anyone does."

She didn't explain that, but after a moment added rather bitterly, "And Sylphara of the Mountain-Breezes has *adopted* those *Líonar* guys, even though *we're* Her *descendants.*"

Amanita's people were descended from a *Goddess?*

That seemed... incredible.

On the other hand, *Thony's* sisters *were* Goddesses now...

Clearly, he was living in a different, um, world than the one he'd been born into.

There had to be a better way to phrase that, but wasn't that the way people said things? The language just wasn't built for people to talk about traveling between worlds.

Thony realized he was distracting himself. And none of this was getting them any closer to dealing with the problem at hand.

If they even could.

He looked at Dae again and straightened up, releasing Amanita and pulling away from her arm as well. He might be able to understand her taste for vengeance a bit better now – given that crazy history – but it wasn't going to help here.

"So... let's say there's some reason why Queen Lilysong – Whomever Else She might Be – can't keep Valderon Raven's Wing and his people out of the Fairy Wood," he began.

Dae nodded, just watching him.

"Well, then... what are our options? We can't just let him *do* that," Thony finished a little lamely.

The mercenette flopped down on her butt in front of him. "Well, as I see it, there really isn't a lot that three kids can really *do* on our own–"

Thony glared at her. "There has to be *something.*"

She gave him a reproving look. "Let me finish, would you? We might not *be* alone. There's the Bard and her friends. It sounded like they're reporting to someone. My suggestion would be to talk to her and her friends and see if we can join in with their plans."

That... seemed eminently reasonable.

"Why would they tell *us* anything?" Amanita asked, her tone still bitter. "We're just *kids,* remember?"

Dae gave her a sympathetic look. "Well, yes. But *I'm* a member of the Guild. Certified, registered, and all that jazz. I don't know if *Julanna Silversea,*" her eyes seemed to glow with a certain overdone enthusiasm at the idea of talking to the woman, "or this Davril guy, or the Daphne they kept mentioning, will realize what that means. But *Istevan* should. I'm pretty sure *he's* a mercenary, too. *He'll* know what it means that I'm a graduate of Sonoro's – he might not like that I'm so young, but he'll take me seriously. And *he* should be able to convince the others."

She hesitated, looking at Amanita. "It... might help if we tell them who you are."

The other girl's fists clenched again. "No... no, we can't. Even if Raven'sWing isn't heading west... I can't do that to... to everyone at home." She looked at Thony and then back at Dae. "I can't risk him deciding to jump on a different opportunity." She made a face. "Besides, if we *did* tell them, they'd be likely to just try to get me – *us* – out of the way where we couldn't be hurt *or* be helpful."

Thony frowned, but Dae just nodded.

"All righty then," the mercenette said decisively. "Let's go get some sleep. Nothing's going to happen today or tomorrow. Darjil is close to a ten-day ride away – or over two week's march on foot. And it sounds like there's something weird about the troops they've impressed there, which is probably why he says it'll take them three weeks.

"I'll run down to the Mercenaries' Guild-house a little later and figure out who Istevan is... and then we can talk to *Julanna Silversea* and the rest."

And with that pronouncement she heaved herself to her feet and started making her way across the roof-scape towards the Inn of the Starred Hoof.

Thony and Amanita scrambled up to follow.

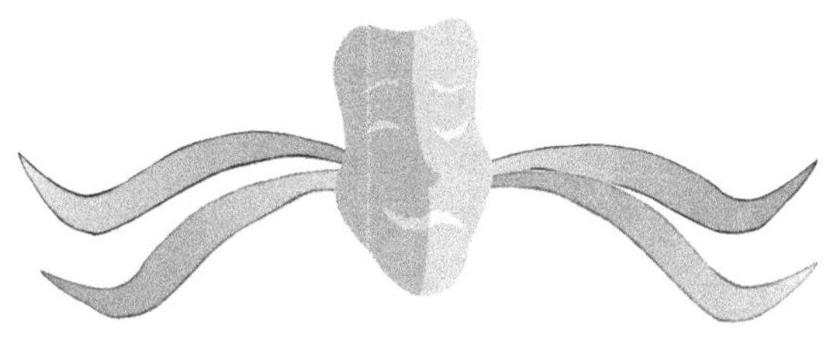

Chapter EIGHT

Swearing Oaths Can Be... Pretty Rude

Thony dragged himself up out of a deep sleep because his stomach was growling.

"What're you up to?" he asked after stepping down the hall for a few minutes to use the 'facilities.' Thank goodness this inn was better equipped than the one down in Aldyrwald's village – guests there had to rely on chamberpots.

"Porridge is on the hearth," Amanita said absently.

The hearth was cold. They'd banked the fire last night before going out on their escapade, putting a huge chunk of firewood *(and where did the wood come from out here on the plains anyhow?)* on to smoulder without going out. It generated a great deal less heat than a blaze, but it also didn't smoke terribly and it didn't draw cold air in from under the door as badly. Not to mention that, from Thony's mountain-bred perspective, it was rather too warm for a full blaze.

The porridge was cold. Thony dipped an unenthusiastic spoon into it and scooped up a gluey, heavy chunk. Without much hope, he checked under the lids of several small pots. To his surprised delight there were chopped nuts of two different kinds, honey, jam, and some small chunks of dried fruit.

Curiously, he sampled everything before mixing in one of the kinds of nuts and all the other things. Even cold porridge would be edible with enough other stuff in it.

"What are these?" he asked Amanita, holding out the nuts he'd decided were interesting, but didn't belong mixed in with the other stuff. They were soft and had a stronger flavor.

She glanced over from where she was seated at the table. "Hmmn? Oh, some sort of ground-nut."

Ground-nut. Thony had no idea what that meant, but wasn't sure how to ask. Nuts grew on trees.

"So, what are you doing?" he asked again, giving up on asking about the other nut or what kind of jam could possibly be *orange.*

Amanita didn't look like she'd slept for very long. There were dark circles under her eyes and she looked like she was propping her head up with one hand because it would fall down if she didn't.

"Transferring the marks from the map," she said wearily. "I dug through your bags to find the ink. Sorry."

She didn't sound terribly sorry, but Thony buried his irritation. The ex-stablegirl wasn't usually the most self-sacrificing person, but she clearly felt very strongly about this. He stood up with his bowl of cold, fruit-and-nut-and-jam-and-honey-laden porridge and came to look over her shoulder.

"Good job," he said clinically. Master Eswith's lessons in Geography had ensured that Thony could read maps *(though* *why they'd bothered, since he wasn't supposed to **go** anywhere had never been clear to him).* There had been drawing and drafting lessons mixed in there somewhere as well, so he could probably copy the map accurately if he wanted and he could certainly appreciate someone else doing the same.

She looked up at him a little blearily. "I wish I could get a copy of this home to my grandmother. She should know... *She* could do something about this mess. Maybe. Our military isn't very big and it's all defensive. Two fronts to defend..."

Her voice trailed off, and Thony realized her eyes had drifted shut and her head was nodding sharply as if about to fall off the supporting hand.

With a sigh, he set down his bowl and hauled her out of the chair. "Go to bed. We can't get anything useful done or decided if you're not awake enough to think."

She was apparently too tired even to argue – which said something right there. "Thanks. You're a good friend. Wish we could get word to your parents, too."

She was sleepy enough... Thony hesitated only an instant to wrestle with his conscience.

"Not sure Papa could put together enough people to fight off an invasion of this size even if we could. But you think your grandmother could?"

Amanita mumbled something about a 'long history' and 'damned *Líonar*' as she snuggled into her pillow. Which wasn't terribly useful.

Thony tried again. "What about your *parents?* Can't they do anything, instead of letting a little old lady do everything?"

An almost-asleep snort. "Nobody believes *Môthir* can handle things like that, Princess-Heir or not. It's all... on... me..."

And she was out.

Thony just stared at the girl's recumbent form. Amanita turned onto her side and started to snore lightly.

Her mother was the 'Princess-Heir' *(did that mean the Crown Princess?)* of this Pathremir place?

No wonder her grandmother made all the decisions for the family. She must be the queen... of a country where women were in charge.

And that made Amanita... what?

She had a brother, she'd sort of admitted while they traveled with Puck. But she'd never so much as hinted at sisters. And she'd always seemed to understand Thony's situation better than he would have expected...

And just now she'd said that no one expected much of her mother.

That it was all on *her.*

The only daughter of the Crown Princess...

She was effectively Crown Princess herself.

Thony thumped himself down heavily into the chair he'd extracted Amanita from. He picked up his almost-forgotten bowl of porridge and began to eat rather mechanically, his mind still churning through what he'd just learned.

Amanita, who had worked in the kitchens and stables in Aldyrwald, was a *princess.*

And Heir to her own country.

How... weird.

No wonder she took everything to do with Pathremir and its history so personally. Thony rather felt that way about Aldyrwald. Not that their history went back so far. Two thousand years, Puck had said. Was that two thousand years *after* they had thrown off their enslavement or did that include that period?

And... Dae seemed to know all about this.

It was... a great deal to think about, and none of it particularly *useful* information right now. Amanita's title didn't mean a great deal more than his own at the moment, after all.

Though if she was willing to *own* it...

No, Thony had to agree with her. The risk of Valderon Raven'sWing – or Captain Shalladra – getting wind of a missing princess wandering around in their territory and deciding to capture her was just too high. Even if they didn't intend to invade her homeland, doubtless there would be some use they could make to leverage her against her... grandmother, the Queen of Pathremir.

Was that the *nice* grandmother or the *awful* one? Thony wondered.

He traced the distance between Flowerdust and Pathremir on the map thoughtfully. A month of travel indeed. That looked like a month by horse, even if most of it was plains. There were only two roads marked as leading up into the mountain-kingdom, neither one a direct route from here...

To distract himself as much as anything, he pulled the pile of not-really-love-letters over and began reading through them.

An hour or so later when Dae poked her head in, he was ready to freak out.

Seeing the sleeping... princess, Dae gestured to him to come out of the room. She looked rather disheveled, but pleased with herself.

Thony joined her in the corridor and they went into Dae's room.

"So how did it go?" he asked. He wasn't sure if he should wait until Amanita was awake to share what he'd learned. He could hold off on freaking out until then.

He hoped.

Dae grinned at him, her expression restored to the happy-go-lucky type she'd sported most of yesterday. *(The phrase reminded him of Midele Featherspray and Girona Starshine... they'd used that term, one or the other of them...)*

"I was right," the mercenette informed him proudly. "He's called Istevan Highblade, but apparently this isn't the first time he's gotten mixed up in this kind of thing, so he's got a bit of a nickname around the Guild as Istevan *Sly*blade. He's a graduate of Sonoro's, too," she added, "but he's old – like over *thirty*."

"And Captain Shalladra?" Thony asked. "You thought she was probably a mercenary, too."

Dae nodded. "She is. Or, well, she *was*. Or she *will be* a *was*. Eventually."

This was confusing even for Dae.

"What," Thony wasn't even sure how to ask.

The mercenette gestured him to sit on the bed while she combed her hair and put it back up in the half-ponytail that seemed to be her preferred style. The young prince had to admit it suited her face as well as doing the job of keeping her hair out of her eyes. She was fairly pretty, when he got a chance to look at her.

Why in – well, *all* the worlds – had she decided to become a mercenary? And at such a young age?

"Shalladra's account has been suspended," Dae was explaining. "By the local Guild-house anyways, although right now there's no real way to get the word out to the rest of the Guild, Evrien says – why are you looking at me like that?"

"Like what?" Thony asked a little defensively.

She narrowed her eyes at him. "Like you just suddenly decided I'm a little kid and need to be protected?"

He steeled himself a bit. "Well, you *are* just a kid. I mean, I'm sure you can do great when you're guarding some other kid, and clearly you can handle traveling alone... but a *war–*"

"*I'm* the one *trained* for this. *You're* the civilian–"

"I'm not arguing that," Thony said quickly. "I don't think *any* of the three of us should be out here."

"Oh. Hmmn." Dae looked at him suspiciously.

"Not me, not you, but especially not the *Crown Princess of Pathremir,*" he emphasized.

The mercenette folded her arms and shifted her weight onto her left hip.

"Well. She's not that, actually. Not *exactly.*"

"But *eventually,*" he copied what she had said a moment ago. "And she's potentially at a greater risk than the rest of us because of it. We need to get her out of here."

Dae cocked her head thoughtfully. "That... makes a great deal of sense. Though you're in the same sort of position, it sounds like."

Thony shook his head. "Not *here*. Not *now*. My title doesn't matter to Raven'sWing."

"It could. If he's using the Fairy Wood to get to *your* homeworld, you could be just as valuable a hostage as Amanita."

Thony winced as she used the word he'd been trying to avoid, and Dae's eyes widened in amazement.

Unrelated amazement, as it turned out.

"I can't believe I just said that. I can't believe all the stories about the Fairy Wood are actually *true* and I'm standing here talking to a... a *boy* from another world."

She paused. "Wait. *Are* you a boy? Are boys boys and girls girls on your world?"

Thony rolled his eyes. "Yes."

Dae raised an eyebrow. "Are we actually *sure* of that? I mean, the unicorn chose *you* and you *were* dressed up like a unicorn-maiden when I met you."

"What do you want me to do? Strip naked?" Thony growled, feeling his face flaming. "Amanita said you people use the word 'maiden' for boys and girls both."

Dae sniggered. "Ooops. That was good marketing on her side. Too bad I ruined it."

Thony covered his face with his hands. He could feel Twinklestar's alarm from down in the stable. The unicorn and horse had snoozed most of yesterday and last night and he hadn't yet realized Thony was awake.

"Or maybe it's true in *Pathremir,*" Dae mused, lifting one hand from her folded arms to tap her lips. "They're awfully different up there."

The young prince was slightly distracted. "You mean matriarchies aren't common?"

Now both of Dae's eyebrows went up. "Did she tell you they were?"

Thony thought about that. "No, I guess not. She just always seemed annoyed that Aldyrwald was patriarchal. We – Wes and I, he's our other friend – we didn't believe that there could really be a country run by *girls.*" His blush was receding as they moved away from Dae's uncomfortable curiosity.

"And you told *her* that?" Dae looked fascinated – the way someone might be if they saw a wagon rolling down a hillside without a driver.

"Um, no, not exactly..." Thony decided it was time to beat a strategic retreat. "Did you find out anything else while you were gone?"

Dae flopped onto the bed next to him. The room was something like half the size of the one he was sharing with Amanita, so there was only the bed. The wall next to the bed looked like it might be the chimney for the hearth downstairs, and was likely the only source of heat.

"Let's see... I told you about Istevan *Sly*blade and Shalladra. Her *nom du guerre* isn't actually 'Icicleblood' by the way. It's Stillheart. Which is probably irrelevant, but still..." The mercenette shook her head, apparently to get *herself* back on track. She was, quite possibly, the most distractable person Thony had ever met. "Anyways, the current Guildhouse-Keeper is a woman named Evrien Quickfoot. She's not so quick now – she's literally ancient, like sixty or something. Anyways, she's not supposed to be in charge here. She just sort of got stuck here. She was heading back to the school *she* trained in, Arazia's Academy at Arms in the Mountains of Koitan, to become a teacher and was just passing through when the Raven troops took over the town."

As Dae paused to take a breath, Thony tried to get a question in.

"Did Shalladra go to one of these training places?"

The mercenette looked thoughtful. "I'm not sure. I didn't ask Evrien." She frowned fiercely. "She's not *acting* like she did, for sure."

"What do you mean?" Thony wanted to know.

"*Well,*" Dae said, "for one thing, she doesn't seem to respect the autonomy of the Guild. Even most kings and queens know not to try to force Guild members into joining their armies. But Evrien says Shalladra went through the Guildhouse like a plague – people either joined up or were put to the sword. And she's kept snapping up any others that have come to town randomly in the month or so since she took over. Apparently, she left Evrien behind because she's so old, but she even forced the guy who *was* our Guildhouse-Keeper, Tethro Fishglitter, to join up."

She seemed particularly incensed about that.

Thony frowned. "If she forced trained warriors to join her troops – wouldn't they just defect as soon as they were able? Or are her troops good enough to force them to stay?"

"Not hardly!" Dae said indignantly. Then she wilted a little. "No, they can't be. Evrien says that the Raven troops are just a weird mix of local militias and the bodyguards of local merchants and nobles... and a handful of actual soldiers from one army or another. We're assuming Raven's Wing has kept the actual trained armies together.

"But the mercenaries have stayed true for a couple of reasons. One is that all the mercenaries – *other* than our friend Istevan – who have been taken this way have disappeared. Evrien says that she *thinks* they were sent east to the main body of troops. Presumably enough people were sent along to keep them under guard along the way – she says there were a lot more Raven troops with Shalladra when she got here."

Thony nodded to himself. That squared with some of the things he'd been reading in Valderon Raven's Wing's letters to his captain. It was kind of frustrating, reading only the letters Shalladra had *received* and having to *intuit* what she had told her boss...

"You said there was a second reason?" Thony asked, kind of dreading the answer. Some of the *other* things suggested in those letters...

But what Dae said wasn't at all what he'd been thinking.

"It's... kind of a mess," the mercenette told him with a certain reluctance. "A mercenary who screws up royally – gets a bad reputation and it's hard to find a job–" which she would know... "but a mercenary who reneges on her sworn oath – *even* if that oath is made under duress – is pretty much done. No one will ever hire her again. For *any* reason."

Thony was horrified. "So, if those men–"

"*And* women," Dae added glumly.

"*And* women – if they gave their oaths to a murdering sorcerer who's trying to conquer the whole world and maybe *all* the worlds – even if they thought he was the worst dude *ever*–"

"They'd feel like they had to stick it out," Dae confirmed. "A lot of them anyways. Most of them. Of us." Clearly, she'd been thinking this through since she talked to this Evrien woman. Though it wasn't entirely clear what she had decided *she* would do if faced with the conundrum.

"And they'd follow his orders?" Thony demanded. "Even if they were *horrible, unethical, cruel* orders?"

Dae looked down at the scuffed toes of her boots. "Yeah. Probably." She looked at him out of the corner of her eye. "You don't have any idea what it's like to be washed-up mercenary, Thony–"

He launched himself off the bed to pace back and forth alongside it, agitatedly. "I know what *ethics* are! Don't *you* people?"

Dae looked up, glaring at him, and pulled her toes out of his path. "I know what it's like to be *poor,* Your Royal Highness! Do *you*? Do you know what it's like not to know how you're going to get a meal today? And you didn't have one yesterday, and you only have a *shot* at getting one tomorrow? Do you know what it's like to have your parents *abandon you* on the doorstep of someone, praying they have a kind heart – or at least that they'll feed you? Do you know–?"

She shut up suddenly and pulled her knees up in front of herself, wrapping her arms around them, her face grim.

"I can't blame any of those guys," she said in a tight voice. "Because if they haven't managed to bank enough savings to see them through the *rest* of their *lives*... pretty much the only openings for a washed-up mercenary are day-labor and begging. And I've heard that even day-labor is hard to find once they find out what you did and why you aren't doing it again. There's no honorable retirement, teaching at the school where you trained, no cottage and garden where you can try and live out your days... no wealth and notoriety... Just everyone who ever took a chance on you being disappointed and pretending you don't exist and eking out an *existence* – not even a *life*..."

She seemed on the verge of tears.

Thony stopped pacing, and looked at her, his heart softening. "No. I don't know those things. But you're not a helpless little kid now, Dae. You have the ability to *save* helpless little kids, with all your mad skills. And what Raven'sWing is doing..."

He closed his eyes and shook his head. "I started reading those letters and... it's *bad*, Dae. Those mercenaries who got taken away – even if they didn't give their oaths, they may have been *enchanted* to obey Raven'sWing. Apparently, he's been able to do that to one person at a time for just about forever, but he's gotten hold of some new kind of magick that is letting him enchant *masses* of people. He's gotten it to work partially in some other places, but the letter two before the one we all looked at last night says he got it work all the way on the whole population of the city of Darjil."

Dae looked as shocked as he felt himself.

"He says..." Thony swallowed hard. "He says in that letter that it was a mess because he ended up enchanting everyone right down to the newborn babies. And that that wasn't *useful* because they can't march. Or follow directions."

"So... what did he *do* with all the babies and toddlers?" Dae asked in a small voice.

Thony shook his head again. "Or the little kids, or the old people and the sick or lame or blind or... whatever? I don't know. The next one has a brief mention that they are working out the details, but it's more about the delays in setting their Grand Plan against the Fairy Wood into motion than anything else. And then that last one..."

"When he said they were on their way," Dae finished for him. "Did you get any idea *why* he thinks he can traverse the Fairy Wood?"

Thony floated a hand and tilted it side to side slightly. "A little bit. There's definitely *some* reason, but either he'd told Shalladra in person or he doesn't want her to know. He's very cagey about committing it to paper. And actually..." He hesitated. "I'm not entirely certain he means to invade *other* worlds or just use the Fairy Wood to move around in *this* one."

Dae's hands flew up to her mouth. "Oh, Gods. If that works... if he can come out where he intends to... there are pieces of it all *over* the world if the stories are right."

Thony nodded. "That's what he implies. I get the feeling he might not *actually* realize it *actually* goes to *other* worlds."

"Well... that's a relief," Dae suggested.

"Yes and no," Thony said. "He could *discover* that it does. Or he could have less control than he thinks he does and come out in, say, *Aldyrwald,* without intending to." Or Eyola, he thought, but didn't say. "And then, well, he's a conqueror with an army at his back..."

Dae nodded grimly. "Do you think Her Highness has had enough of a nap? She should probably hear all this. Yours and mine both."

"Hmmn." Thony wasn't looking forwards to telling her. Amanita had been so guiltily relieved that Pathremir was safe, even though Aldyrwald might be at a greater risk.

"Maybe we could let her have a little longer?" he suggested. "And you could explain all these mercenary surnames to me? They don't seem like family names the way you're using them. And they clearly aren't *descriptive*."

The chocolaty-brown eyes of Dae *Goldeneyes* twinkled with amusement. "No, we choose our own. Each one is supposed to say something about who we think we are. Not like those crazy knights over in Dawil, who let *priestesses* come up with a name for them."

Thony let this pass, since the impression he was getting of the faraway country was inconsistent and how they named their knights was highly irrelevant.

"So, some guy actually picked the name *'Fishglitter'* for *himself?*" he asked, though it was Dae's surname that he was actually more curious about. "I was thinking it must be a cruel joke that stuck."

Dae shrugged. "I actually don't know. Tethro's sort of famous in the Guild. He's the youngest mercenary ever to give up being a fighter in order to take care of a Guild-house. And in a super-boring place like Flowerdust – everyone has a theory, but I was actually coming here to ask him about it. You know, youngest mercenary ever, youngest House-Keeper ever... figured we'd bond."

There was something evasive about the way she said it...

"So how old is he?" Thony asked.

Dae could keep her secrets, even if she'd managed to ferret out most of his and Amanita's. She's shown him rather more of her own insides than he thought she'd meant to already.

"Oh, really old," Dae replied. "Like twenty-eight or something."

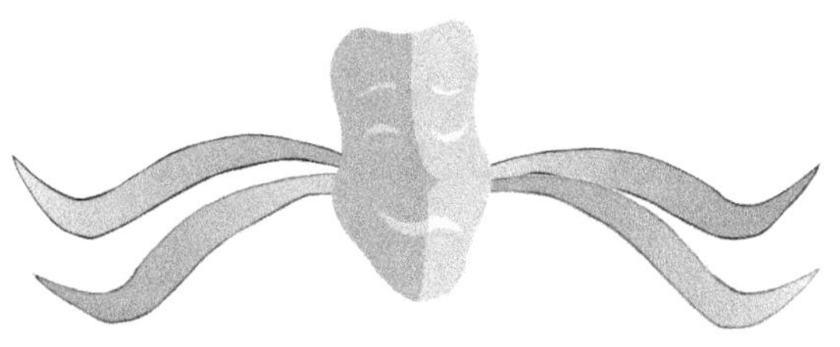

Chapter NINE

Hey, Baby

AMANITA WAS JUST WAKING UP when the other pair came back into the room. The sun was setting, and they could hear Julanna Silversea warming up downstairs.

Minstrel's surnames, Dae had explained, were bestowed upon them by their masters at the school they lived in and were based on the content or title or something of the song they created as a masterwork. This gave the aspiring musician some control over what they were called, and though they could still get stuck with something awful, it was possible to get everyone to switch over to calling them something else if they did something particularly dramatic.

Though that could be good or bad, and she had a number of funny stories about famous people *(not just minstrels)* who had ended up with even worse nicknames than whatever they had started with.

And, properly, Julanna Silversea was a *Bard,* not a minstrel. There was supposed to be a capitol letter on that, and Dae said the word the way Thony's Mama emphasized all of her Overly Dramatic Pronouncements.

Dae was trying to explain the differences between different categories of musicians to Thony as they came back into the room he shared with Amanita. Supper had been waiting on a tray in the hallway, and they brought it in with them.

"I did *not* mean to sleep so long," Amanita said, covering a yawn, as Thony set the tray on the table. "We've lost a whole day."

Out the window behind her, the sky was turning majestic shades of purple streaked with pinky-gold clouds in ragged rows.

"We worked all *night* long," Dae said philosophically. She eyed the two-person portions and settings on the tray a little enviously. "I suppose I should go down and find my own dinner. Thony can catch you up on everything."

She started opening the door again.

Thony tried not to cringe at that idea. "Yeah, I suppose–"

There was a sound of a door slamming open below and crashing pottery and exclamations that verged the threshold between fearful and indignant.

Thony yanked Dae back into the room as Amanita ripped up the loose floorboard.

The mercenette managed to get in a whisper of "Cool!" before they all crouched over the narrow gap over the taproom.

"–enemy of the state," Shalladra's mellow voice was saying cattily.

"Shalladra, no!" Istevan sounded winded, and as the three young people peered through the tiny space, they could see that he was kneeling on the floor, one hand pressed to his ribs, the other holding him more or less upright.

Julanna was behind him, pressed against the wall, her stool upended and her instrument hugged tight against her bosom.

"What did you call me, Lieutenant?" the Captain purred.

"Captain," he gasped. "She's done nothing–"

"*Famous Bards* don't play miserable dirty little taverns in dead-end towns for nothing, Lieutenant," Shalladra informed him. She stepped into view, but there was nothing new – she looked as sharp as before. Her smirk was perhaps a bit more pronounced – and triumphant. "The woman is clearly a spy. Take her away," she said over her shoulder, and a pair of blue-uniformed Raven troops – both men and rather large and husky ones – came forwards with chains.

The instrument – Thony still couldn't quite tell, but thought it looked more or less like a lute – fell to the ground in a great jangle as Julanna Silversea was cuffed and led away.

"She's not a *spy,* Captain," Istevan tried again once Julanna was gone. "She's just down on her luck. And–"

Captain Shalladra reached down and wrenched the man to his feet with a hand on his upper arm. Istevan wasn't exceedingly tall, but he was taller than his captain and probably outmassed her a fair amount. Thony had to be impressed with both the woman's strength and the nonchalance and lack of seeming effort with which she used it.

She was close enough that Thony could actually see her teeth when she smiled cruelly. Or... he thought he could. But surely the woman didn't have *pointed* teeth?

"You protest so *much,* dear Istevan," the Captain hissed as he curled over what was clearly an aching gut. "I'm near to considering you to be her accomplice instead of her dupe.

Shall I put you a few cells down and see what information I can wring out of you both – Istevan *Sly*blade." She paused. "Or did you think I wouldn't learn about the *other* skills you're so famous for?"

"Shalladra – Captain–"

"Or shall we find a more... *civilized* way of dealing with this? She'll stay in my dungeon and you'll do as I say – keep me happy and *I* won't harm a hair on her head." She paused. "Of course, milord will have his *own* opinion regarding spies when he arrives. And possible collusion with them from within the ranks of his own troops. He doesn't take kindly to treachery, I can assure you. But I *might* find a way to keep from mentioning *you* in my report on the minstrel.. And that's all *you've* ever cared about, isn't it?"

She smiled again, and Thony tried to see her teeth but didn't get any better of a look. "You're too pretty to decorate a gibbet – or a rack. Not that milord mightn't have something more creative to do with you. *And* the minstrel."

Istevan slumped in defeat. "You win. *Captain.*"

"Play nice, Istevan," Shalladra purred, then her voice sharpened. "Atten-*tion,* Lieutenant! Don't ever let me see you groveling in the dirt again, or I'll have you up on charges of conduct unbecoming an officer!"

Istevan forced his long body to straighten, but it clearly pained him. He pulled his arm up into a salute. "Sir, yes, sir!"

"Much better, Istevan. Follow me and we'll – ah – *discuss* the rest of the terms of our little agreement."

Captain Shalladra led off and Istevan followed, limping slightly, but clearly not daring to slouch.

Amanita carefully lowered the floorboard into its place as the other two eased back.

"Well," she said after a moment when they all stared at each other. "That's a thing, I guess."

Dae was looking outraged. "You can't arrest a *Bard*. And especially not *Julanna Silversea!*"

Thony waved a hand in front of both girls. "Bigger problems, ladies. Shalladra may or may not *actually* torture those two – but there's a couple dozen people downstairs, including the innkeeper and his family. *Someone* is going to remember that the Bard had a couple more people in her party."

"Davril and Daphne," Dae breathed.

Thony nodded as Amanita stood up and brushed off her knees.

"We have to let them know!" she declared.

As one, the three young people moved out of the room and to the room on the opposite side as Dae's. Thony knocked.

The man who opened the door wasn't anywhere near as dashing as the black-haired Istevan in his sharp blue uniform. He was... slightly homely, actually, with dusty brown hair, eyes that were in that nameless shade between green and brown that wasn't quite hazel, and a face that was friendly without being terribly interesting. He was slender, rather than muscular and a hair on the short side – so only a couple inches taller than Thony. And he looked much younger than Thony would have guessed from their eavesdropping: he looked only a little older than Pricilla, who had just turned seventeen when Thony had left home (*not that age probably meant anything to Her anymore*).

"Yes?" he asked. His friendly-looking face was closed and wary.

"You're Davril?" Amanita asked, stepping around Thony. "We have some bad news for you. Julanna Silversea was just arrested downstairs. By Captain-Mayoress Shalladra Stillheart."

Davril stumbled back a step in shock. "No! Wait... who *are* you kids?"

He was clearly not someone who undertook espionage for a living with that open, honest face and these obviously-uncalculated reactions.

Thony shook his head. "Friends – or we mean to be anyways."

"It gets worse," Dae said from his other side. "Or maybe better. She named Julanna Silversea an enemy of the state, but it just seemed to be an excuse to arrest her. It looks like the Captain's planning to just keep Julanna Silversea around to use as a lever to make Istevan Highblade do whatever she wants."

Davril looked grim. And scared. "That idiot. I *told* him this was too dangerous–"

Thony interrupted. "And... Valderon Raven'sWing is going to be here in less than a week."

Ten days' ride from Darjil, Dae had said, and Thony had confirmed that on the map. And the letter had been dated from a week ago.

And *now* Davril went utterly white under his deep tan.

"We... we have to get out of here," he said in a very controlled voice. "Now..."

Amanita nodded. "You and – Daphne. We'll help with whatever you need. Where's Daphne?"

She peered in, curiously, because the room was the same size as the one that she and Thony were sharing and there didn't seem to be space for three people.

"I'll get her," Davril said grimly.

He stepped back into the room, letting Thony hold the door, and pulled on a long, hooded cloak before scooping up a sleeping baby in his arms. Very dark red curls made it likely that this was Julanna's child – was the child's hair so dark because Istevan was the father? Thony wondered, but it didn't seem like the time to ask.

"Do you have a place to go?" Dae asked as Amanita wanted to know if they shouldn't pack first.

Davril shook his head as he swept down the corridor and started on the stairs. "I'll figure something out. Getting *out* is the first and most important thing, they've always told me."

"I know a place," Dae offered as the three younger people followed Davril down the stairs.

The taproom had been abandoned. The innkeeper sat glumly behind the bar, staring at a floor that was stained with ale half-soaked into the floorboards and the shards of broken mugs. He appeared to be drowning his sorrows in his own product and hardly seemed to register their presence as they moved between stairwell and main door.

Davril paused for a moment before leaving the building, turning to look back at Julanna's overturned stool.

"Would you..." The man cleared his throat when it came out raspy. "Would one of you collect her *saz,* please? It... was a gift from her father and it's more or less irreplaceable on this side of the world.

"Of course!" Thony hurried over to pick up the stringed instrument. It looked undamaged, but he wasn't all that familiar with musical instruments. He cradled it in his arms nearly as carefully as Davril had the baby.

"Should I go back up for the case?" he asked as he came back over to the others.

The man just shook his head. When Amanita opened the door, they all went out.

Davril paused outside the door, and looked over *(and down)* at Dae. "A place you said? Damn, but I shouldn't be trusting you, I've never met any of you in my life..."

His face was shadowed in the hood, but his voice was anguished.

"It's outside the town," Dae told him. "I saw it on my way in."

There was something not quite open about her statement... Thony brushed it aside. Either he trusted the girl or he didn't, and she'd had plenty of time – and even plenty of *reason* – to turn him and Amanita over to the Raven troops.

"Should we take the equines?" he asked quietly.

Dae looked at Davril. "You don't have horses of your own, do you?"

The man shook his head, his tone laced with anxiety. "Not riding beasts. Stev has his, of course, but she's in the barracks stables. We have a wagon and wagon-horses renting space at the south stables..."

Dae shook her head. "There won't be room for a whole wagon. Let's get your horse and unicorn, Thony."

It took longer than anyone liked to saddle up Silverfoot and – at Dae's suggestion – fasten a blanket around Twinklestar's middle. And then, once both equines were ready, Dae decided that they would be more inconspicuous if they walked the equines out of town, rather than riding them.

This they did, with Thony biting his tongue on complaining about having wasted the time to collect them – Twinklestar was giving him a headache as it was about what an inappropriate hour this was for travel. Amanita was *not* biting her tongue on her own, similar, thoughts, and was maintaining a continual low mutter.

Davril was silent except for making a rather monotonous crooning *hummm,* presumably to keep the baby quiet and sleepy.

And Dae strode ahead blithely.

At a few hundred feet out of town the road went down into a small dip – one of the minor undulations of the flat plain. Dae had them all mount up at this point: Davril and the baby with Amanita on the smooth-gaited Silverfoot, and herself in the pillion-position behind Thony on Twinklestar.

To Thony's relief, the unicorn seemed, at last, to have decided that this was a worthwhile adventure – once he'd seen the baby handed up to Davril on the horse's back, anyways.

The road they traveled seemed familiar, even with all the color of everything bleached out in the moonlight. After several minutes of watching a dark blob ahead grow larger, Thony realized it was the same road they had come in on, and that was the Fairy Wood ahead.

"Dae, are you *sure–?*" he began, trying to keep his voice pitched only for the girl peering around his shoulder.

"I know, Thony," the mercenette said. "But we should have several days to find a way to move them somewhere safer – assuming there *is* anywhere safer."

In the end, they didn't actually enter the Wood, but veered slightly to the east of the grove.

There, they dismounted and led the equines down into a tiny grotto.

A *neigh* welcomed them, and Dae slipped off Twinklestar's butt and ran up to put her arms around the neck of a small horse.

"This is Sandy," she introduced them to her horse. "I brought him out here yesterday morning. I couldn't afford to pay stable fees," she admitted candidly, "and I didn't think the innkeeper at the Starred Hoof would accept me cleaning up the stable in exchange for us staying there."

"I *knew* it hadn't looked that good the first night!" Thony exclaimed.

Dae nodded as she whipped out her little thief's lantern and lit it, uncovering more sides so that it glowed in several directions instead of just in that one, focused beam.

"This spot is just perfect for hiding," she said as she invited them deeper in. "There's a little stream over there – and the bushes and trees make it look like it's dense thicket with no space inside."

"How did *you* find it?" Amanita marveled as Davril settled down with the baby.

Dae shrugged. "It was really more Sandy than me." She looked back at Davril. "I can leave you the lantern, but I'm not sure I'd want to risk a fire, myself, even down in this hollow, since the smoke might give it away. We'll pack up the rest of your stuff and get it out here to you tomorrow. Will the two of you be alright out here until then?"

"Yes..." Davril looked distracted. "I don't suppose you could – no, you're just kids and you've already put yourselves in danger to help us..." His voice trailed off.

But he looked... fragile.

"You need to know what's happened to Julanna and Istevan," Thony interpreted. He glanced at the two girls. "We can do that."

Davril shook his head. "No... no. They'll be fine. And they'd never forgive me if I sent you kids to check on them."

He looked embarrassed to say it – he wasn't all that much older than the three of them, after all.

Amanita – who had somehow ended up with the *'saz'* during the escape – held the instrument out awkwardly towards the man, but her expression was firm.

"*You* wouldn't be sending us anywhere. This is something we're choosing for ourselves. And we're not *little* kids," she added with some asperity. "We're all of us practically adults by age, and Dae and I have both been on our own for awhile now."

"Dae..." Davril looked at the mercenette. "I never got any of your names back there..." He shook his head ruefully. "Stev and Julanna would both have my hide for being so trusting. You can't be *Dae Goldeneyes?*"

The mercenette preened a little. "You've heard of me?"

Davril gave a mirthless snort of laughter. "Nothing you'd be happy with, I'm afraid. When Stev – Istevan – heard about you, he spent a few weeks going on and on about how Sonoro's standards must have fallen since he graduated."

She looked more resigned than miffed. "As if the Fox would ever let that happen."

Davril looked apologetic. "He... may have said something about Sonoro giving over the school to his granddaughter being 'a sign of favoritism and decadence.' In one of his rants."

Dae's lips pursed. "Clearly, he's never *met* Taridanae Foxheart himself, or he'd know better. How old *is* your boy, anyways? Forty?"

Davril choked on what seemed a genuinely startled laugh. "How could you–? Nevermind. No, Stev's thirty-two."

"He must have left the school right before she took over, then," Dae interpreted. "I started training when I was about four, under the Fox herself. Trust me, I can handle myself."

"That's... not entirely what we heard," Davril demurred. "Through the Guild-house grapevine. There was a certain wardrobe malfunction we heard about at the Royal Court of Canador."

Dae glanced at Thony and Amanita. "The Duchess of Middleveld was kind of asking for it. Drooling all over Prince Harper like that. He was only twelve himself and his bride-to-be was right there."

Thony nodded to himself. That sounded reasonable.

"And an explosion in a cheese-factory in Widdenward," Davril went on, "and several hundred yards of fabric from the neighboring loomhouse were somehow involved. And weren't you on *guard* at the loomhouse?"

Thony and Amanita exchanged a look of interest as Dae lifted her chin. "They hired me to make sure no one walked off with the cloth-of-gold for Queen Raellia's coronation robe. Nothing happened to *that.*"

"And the herd of Ancorea goats that ended up having to be sheared early because their wool somehow *shrank* en route to the market... on their bodies?" Davril looked away as the baby began to stir in his arms, but there was a smirk not quite manifesting on his face.

"We heard that Kamauri Spiralspear and Daennor Cat'sFoot have been trying to track you down," he added as he got little Daphne settled again. How he was going to feed her, Thony had no idea.

"Kamauri thinks she's my big sister," Dae said in an exasperated voice. "It's been *two years* since I graduated. I'm doing *fine.*"

Which sort of contradicted what she'd said before about not being able to afford a room and stabling... But on the other hand, she *had* been doing this for two years...

"Hmmn." Davril looked at her, and his face was serious and worried again. "Just... please be careful. Shalladra has no reason to do damage to Istevan – and all the reason in the world *not* to let Julanna come to harm. But *you three...*"

"Fair enough," Thony said before Dae could argue any further. He put a hand on the backs of both girls and nudged them to get moving. "We need to get back if we're to pack up your stuff and bring it back here tomorrow. You'll need – diapers and food if nothing else, I suppose."

Davril winced. "Yes, we will. And fresh goat's milk if you can get any. Daphne is still mostly nursing and upsetting her tummy with eating all new things won't help us stay hidden... And, kids?" he added as they started making their way out of the copse.

They all looked back, Dae muttering grouchily to herself.

"Thank you," he said in a heartfelt tone. In the dim glow of the lantern, his homely face was almost good-looking as his eyes shone with appreciation. "It's important that we don't let Daphne get taken. And I might not have been able to get her out in time on my own."

Thony just nodded and propelled the girls out of the hollow.

As they made their way to the horses, Amanita asked, "So... just how *do* you make a cheese-factory explode?"

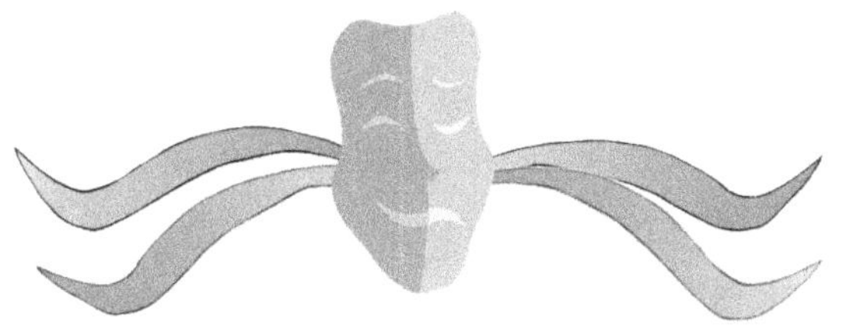

Chapter TEN

The Truth Will Out

SOMEHOW THE GIRLS ENDED UP riding back together on Silverfoot. Amanita had sort of winced at the idea of paying to stable a *fourth* animal, and Dae had left Sandy behind with what looked like only minor regrets.

Thony didn't mind at all. Having Dae hanging over his shoulder and directing which way they were to go had been uncomfortable, to say the least. The girl had a grip of steel, and his collar-bones were still sore, even after he'd tried to discreetly massage his shoulders and neck once they had reached the hidden hollow.

"So, who's this Kamauri-person, and why didn't you tell us someone was after you?" Amanita asked after they were on the road, and not so obviously leaving a hideaway.

Dae heaved a sigh. "Kamauri Spiralspear. She sort of 'adopted' me while she was at Sonoro's. She graduated a year before I did... and I think *she* thought I was going to stay until I was entirely grown up. Even though I was in all the classes right behind hers. They really didn't have anything left for me to *learn*," she added a little defensively. "The Fox said it was time for me to move on as well – though *she* seemed to think I should go to a university or something."

"That still seems like it could cause some issues," Amanita noted. "I've never heard of a mercenary going to a university. Or a twelve-year-old."

"Oh, people retire from the trade and go all the time," Dae said blithely. "Or... maybe not *all* the time. By the time a mercenary has the money to *afford* to go, they generally are old and broken down and just want to retire quietly."

"How old is that?" Thony asked, thinking that sounded pretty awful.

Dae shrugged. "Really ancient. You know, like forty."

He frowned. "Didn't you say the woman looking after your Guildhouse in Flowerdust right now is more like sixty?"

"Yeah, she's practically fossilized," Dae agreed. "She's probably the oldest active mercenary *alive.*"

"Ummm..." Thony began.

"It's a hard job, Thony," Dae said seriously. "You can survive what you're doing as long as you're better and faster than the people you're fighting against – and that usually means *younger.* Older fighters have to be really, really good – and much more crafty. And that's not easy."

"Does that mean you have an advantage or a disadvantage, starting so young?" he wanted to know, and she shrugged again.

"Kinda hard to say. If I don't get injured–" *or die, presumably, but if she wasn't going to say it, neither was he,* "–then I should have more experience than mercenaries who get started at the normal ages... by the time I'm their age. On the other hand, every time you're in a fight you're at risk. And older fighters aren't just older and creakier like other old people – they have scar tissue and maybe things that healed, but not quite right. Things that have to do with how long they've been fighting, not just how old they are."

"So, basically, you're at a disadvantage on size *now,*" Thony summarized a little unwillingly, "and it's not really clear if the early start will compensate at the other end of things."

Dae looked displeased to have it put that way, but nodded.

"That didn't really answer *my* question," Amanita noted over her shoulder – Dae was riding pillion again. "*I* wanted to know more about this Kamauri-chick. And didn't Davril mention someone else?"

"Daennor Cat'sFoot," Dae sighed. "Yes. They've been trying to make me go back to Sonoro's to 'grow up a little' ever since the Canador incident. Which, by the way, worked out *fine,*" she added in an aggrieved tone. "King Ederard fired me, but Harper was so pleased that he gave me a *huge* bonus."

"What exactly happened?" Thony asked in fascination.

Amanita gave him an annoyed look for sidetracking the conversation, but was presumably also interested, since she didn't interrupt.

Dae grinned. "I'd been Harper's bodyguard for about six months when the whole betrothal thing came up. He wasn't too happy about it – Princess Elivia is about ten years older than he is, but she seems nice enough and she's really beautiful. More to the point, his dad – King Ederard – is super old – like Evrien Quickfoot, and no one knows how much longer he's going to last. Harper's mom is the fifth queen and the first one to have a living child make it past toddlerhood."

"That sounds... hmmmn," Thony exchanged a look with Amanita.

"Yeah, assassination," Dae agreed. "Everyone knows, but they couldn't figure out how it was happening. Each of the babies apparently just seemed to have trouble figuring out how to use their muscles. And eventually they couldn't breathe and... *pfft.*"

Her sad expression made up for the rather offhanded way she was describing the loss of those royal infants. Thony was put in mind of how his father, King Bill, had described the children that Mama had miscarried between Joanna and Priscilla. His *brothers and sisters* that had never been born – Thony had known about the miscarriages, but had never thought about them that way until that conversation the day before he had left Aldyrwald.

During that discussion, Papa had looked like a bit of himself – and likely a bit of Mama, too – had crumbled with each loss. But they'd had Joanna, and they loved each other dearly... and divorce wasn't a simple thing for royalty. But if they *hadn't* had a living child and loved each other...

Had this King Ederard loved his various queens? Thony wondered. And... what had happened with the other four? Had they been 'set aside' – honorably retired to a country estate, the marriage voided so that the king could wed again? What about their families? Surely each queen was also a princess and there were treaties with her homeland that would be dependent on the marriage remaining intact. At least, that was the way it worked in the Mountain Region back home...

"There's some suspicions that King Ederard is being slowly poisoned as well," Dae went on soberly. "He's having muscle problems, too – and that's been getting worse since he was a young man, from the whispers I heard. Harper seems fine, but who knows how much longer before the country is his to rule – his mom is sweet, but she's just country nobility. She wasn't picked for anything but another try at having babies, and she just isn't all that interested in government."

Thony shifted uncomfortably in his seat on Twinklestar's back. This sounded a bit too close to his own problems. Twinklestar noted that he was well out of that mess for the time being and should enjoy his freedom as a unicorn-maiden.

Amanita nodded thoughtfully. "So, this princess would be the *real* power. And someday the kid would grow up and be old enough to marry her... and she'd have made sure he wasn't a stupid jerk about it all. But how did this all get mixed up with the Duchess What's-her-face?"

Dae sighed. "The Duchess of Middleveld. Lascha Lohrstorser. She was about sixteen herself at the time, actually. She'd grown up in the castle, bossing Harper around, and I *guess* she'd assumed he was going to marry *her* when they both grew up. I know *he* thought that, too, and he wasn't exactly thrilled about it, but figured he didn't get to pick and choose. Her Lord-Regent – her uncle, who's King Ederard's younger brother – had given over guardianship of her to the king for some reason, and it seemed likely that reason was to position her as the princess-consort-to-be.

"So, anyways, the marriage negotiations had all been done privately, of course, but they were doing the big, fancy presentation ceremony and betrothal thing in public. And Lascha was all set up to ruin it – she'd started hanging all over Harper every chance she got – and kept trying to dismiss me so they could have *'alone time'*–"

"Oooh-la-la," Amanita said sarcastically, and Dae nodded.

"Yeah, well, you can't dismiss the royal bodyguard, but she didn't *know* that was my job. Technically, even Harper couldn't dismiss me, but we had a system worked out... what?"

"How could she not know you were his bodyguard?" Thony asked.

Amanita snorted. "She means she dressed up like a noble and pretended, right, Dae?"

The mercenette nodded. "I was supposed to be a cousin of Harper's from his mother's side – it's some obscure noble family from the back-of-beyond of their country, so no one at Court was familiar enough to call me out. And since I was supposed to be *'family,'* and even *closer* family than Lascha – the king's brother was her mom's sister's husband – she couldn't *officially* tell me to go. She could just be snide, and try to get me to leave on my own. Which, of course, I wasn't going to do no matter what she came up with. Harper apologized for her behavior a lot," Dae added with a wry voice, "but I told him it was fine. That was what they were paying me for, after all. And if it spared him some of her nastiness, it was fine by me."

"This Lascha sounds like a piece of work," Amanita noted as they paused for a moment at the edge of the city to dismount. It wouldn't be very effective to have walked the equines out to avoid attention and then ride them back to the Inn of the Starred Hoof, after all.

"Oh, she is," Dae agreed. "Anyways, she was going to do some crappy thing like throw herself into the middle of the presentation ceremony and swear her undying love for Harper or something – which wouldn't have *changed* anything, I mean all the papers were signed and all – but it would have made things awfully awkward for him and Princess Elivia."

"So, you stepped on her dress just before she could do it," Amanita surmised. "But you said the entire skirt tore off, *and* the petticoats?"

"And she was wearing this skimpy, lacy underwear," Dae winced and grinned at the same time. "*And* everyone could see she had King Everard's name tattooed in a little heart on her butt. Which caused a *huge* scandal, let me tell you. Nobody was happy. She and I both got sent out of the Court in disgrace – except for her it was real, and for me it was losing my job."

"Then who's guarding your prince?" Thony frowned.

"He's not *my* prince," Dae retorted, then softened. "But he *is* my friend. And I was worried about that, but Princess Elivia declared that clearly King Everard's Court wasn't a healthy place for her fiancé to grow up, so she and her parents insisted that Harper come to *their* kingdom for a few years. And she promised me she would keep him safe and that he'd have a chance to really be more of a kid, rather than the 'Precious Hope and Heir to the Realm'."

Thony shifted uncomfortably again, thinking of Mama and Papa. "That seems kind of hard on his parents."

Dae shrugged. "I can't fix *everything*. Harper was really relieved, and he seemed excited to go. It's far enough away that it would be awkward for whomever killed his brothers and sisters to get at him, but not so far away that he and his parents can't visit back and forth occasionally."

"It sounds like you did a good job there," Amanita commented as they dismounted at the edge of town to walk the equines in the rest of the way. "But that doesn't seem to be the story going around... wait, if you were undercover, how do Davril and Istevan and all even know about this?"

"How could you even fake being a noble that well?" Thony wanted to know.

Amanita rolled her eyes. "Really, Thony? It's not like you're all that different."

He narrowed his eyes at her. "I suppose if anyone would know, *you* would."

She glared back at him. "What's *that* supposed to mean?"

"It means I know who you are, *Your Highness.*" He said it as sarcastically as he could, to confuse anyone who might be listening. Thony was still a bit put out that she hadn't wanted *him* to know, but he agreed with her reasons for not wanting to spread it around more generally. "Not that it matters to *me.*"

"Oh." Amanita seemed rather floored by that for a moment. Then she looked hard at Dae.

Who held up her hands in a warding gesture. "Don't look at me. I didn't tell him. He figured it all out on his own."

"I did," Thony confirmed when Amanita looked back at him.

They all walked in silence for a moment before Amanita looked at him sideways. "You're not going to make this all *weird* now, or something, are you?"

He frowned. "What do you mean?"

"Because of your Quest," she explained. "Because you're looking for a... an... ummm... And I'm a... well..."

Was *that* why she hadn't told him? Thony laughed aloud.

"*Gods,* no. That sounds like a disaster on wheels."

Amanita managed to look offended and relieved at the same time. Dae frowned at them both, clearly trying to sort that out.

"I mean," Thony tried to elaborate while still keeping in mind that they were walking along a public street. Even if it was getting pretty late at night. Or maybe that was early in the morning by now. "If I understand it, you're in kind of the same position as I am, except at one remove. You have to go back home, eventually, just like I do. And Pathremir and Aldyrwald are nowhere near close enough for anything like that to work."

That wasn't the *only* reason he wouldn't consider her as the princess he was looking for... but it was a fair enough reason to explain his reaction. He hoped.

Trying to explain that he liked her as a friend, but that the idea of spending the rest of his life with her made his brain feel like it was exploding would certainly *not* help. Or that her taste for vengeance kind of weirded him out. Or that she had a streak of recklessness as wide as an ox-cart. Or...

Just... no.

On the other hand, what if *she*...?

"Oh, good," Amanita said with a great sigh of relief. "You're a good friend, Thony, but you have all these stupid ideas about *'what boys can do'* and *'what girls should do.'* And you're way too cautious. Even if that idea wasn't totally gross."

Apparently, *she* didn't have any such compunctions about sparing *his* feelings.

Which should be somewhere on his list, too, probably.

Dae had apparently reasoned out what they were talking about. "Is *that* why the two of you have been pussyfooting around each other? Oh my God. That is just *too* funny. Though I can see your point. Both your points, actually."

Her smirk at Thony made him guess that she had an idea of all the things he hadn't wanted to say aloud.

He hoped she'd keep her thoughts on that to herself.

"Twinklestar says it doesn't matter anyways, since I'm his unicorn-maiden," Thony said.

For some reason that made Dae wince. "Um, yeah, about that..."

She stopped speaking as they entered the stables.

"About what?" Thony asked.

"Well... you *see*... ummm..."

In the relative privacy, Amanita rolled her eyes. "Dae, spit it out. Whatever it is."

"My friend Kamauri, the one who keeps trying to 'help' me? Um... she's a unicorn-maiden, too."

Well, *that* boggled Thony's mind. Though now the name 'Spiralspear' made a great deal more sense...

Twinklestar's ears had perked up in interest.

"What does that have to do with the price of rice in Eládaí?" Amanita asked impatiently.

Dae looked at her sideways as she refilled the equines' water trough.

"Well... That other guy, Daennor? The one who's been helping Kamauri look for me? Her letters suggest that he's kind of hoping to convince her that she and Rainsparkle should part ways. And *his* letters–"

"Waitaminute," Thony interrupted. "Are you telling me these people are trying to *hunt you down* and you're *writing letters back and forth?* How are you even *doing* that?"

The mercenette shrugged. "We send them through the Guildhouses, of course."

"But how do they know where to send your mail?" Thony wanted to know. "And how do they get there ahead of you – *and* these other guys?"

Dae shrugged again. "I don't know. Magick, I suppose. Something to do with the Guildhouse-Keepers. Though Evrien didn't seem to know anything more than that there *were* letters waiting for me–"

Amanita's eyebrows flew up at this. "You *just* got letters from the people chasing you? So, you know where they are?"

"Um... well, they sent the letters from Indistran..." Dae looked like she was hedging.

Amanita narrowed her eyes. "You know more than that."

"Not because of the *letters,*" Dae said, then her eyes widened. "Oops."

Thony sighed and finished putting out oats and fresh straw for his unicorn. "Twinklestar wants to know just how close this unicorn-lady and her mercenary are."

Amanita glanced over at them. "How does he know it's a girl unicorn?"

It was Thony's turn to shrug. "He says Rainsparkle is a filly's name."

"Hunh." Amanita looked at Twinklestar. "I thought you were all sweet on Puck's fairy-horse. Won't Chillabiaen be annoyed with you?"

Twinklestar tossed his head and whinnied.

Thony winced, since his ear was *right there*. "He says it's a stallion's right to collect a variety of mares." He noticed both girls glaring at him and waved his hands in front of his chest in a warding gesture. "That's *his* comment, not mine. Equines are different than humans. Even *centaurs* are different, according to Jeremy, and they're *half* human."

Amanita looked thoughtful about that. "That's true... Dae, you still haven't told us where these 'friends' of yours are."

Dae sighed. "They might be in Flowerdust by now. Though Evrien said they hadn't been by the Guildhouse yet."

"*What??!*"

Both of the others had exclaimed at once.

"Well, we have a couple of days in a town before we have to–"

"*Not* what I meant," Amanita said. "You have people trying to *track you down* and *take you away* and they might be *right here* and you didn't *tell us?*"

Dae shrugged a little sheepishly. "I mean, once they find out I have another job, and it's legit, it's not like they should feel like they have to do anything. Our 'little misunderstandings' have only occurred when I *don't* have a job. And, well, when *they* don't have jobs, so they have time to go looking for me."

"'Little misunderstandings'?" Thony asked, just as Amanita demanded, "*What* job?"

"They've caught up with me a couple of times," Dae admitted. "And I had to get away. It got... noisy a few times. Or, um, wet. Or... gooey. And my *job* is helping the Lost Princess of Pathremir get home again. I *assume* you'll pay me a fair wage for my work as a bodyguard. Once we get there. Or your grandmother will."

Amanita looked rather outraged... and then rather thoughtful.

Thony wanted to know these *other* stories of Dae's escapades. *Gooey?!?*

And... he wanted to get some sleep. Their shared escapade of last night was still catching up with him.

"Let's go pack up Davril's things," he suggested. "Tomorrow, we can take it all out to him and then figure out what our next step is."

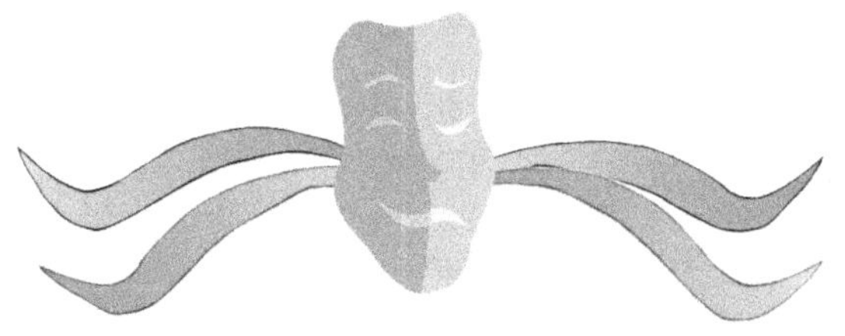

Chapter ELEVEN

An Unexpected Proposition

BY MORNING, THE TAPROOM OF the inn looked much better. They'd decided to come down for breakfast to check on things. Apparently, the innkeeper – or his family, including that little boy, Clarick – had recovered from the intrusion enough to clean up. The floor wasn't sparkling, but then it hadn't been before, either.

Clarick's dad still looked morose, presumably because an inn where a Bard was arrested wasn't likely to be looked well on by other potential patrons, or so Dae told Thony. But Clarick's mom's cooking wasn't affected and breakfast was pretty decent.

The little boy had a message for them as well.

"Jost said to tell all of you that he has some news. You," he indicated Amanita, "are to meet him near the pear-seller's stall in the market."

"What kind of news?" Amanita wanted to know.

Clarick shrugged. "His boy didn't tell *me*. Normally they don't talk to me at all, actually."

"Why not?" Thony frowned.

Another shrug. "I don't live on the streets. Papa made sure Magritte and I are learning how to read and write and figure. That's enough to make us too *different* from most of the street-kids. Jost looks at things his own way, though. He says maybe someday we'll need his help. Or maybe someday we'll all be grown up and he and his kids will need jobs – and I'll have the inn. Or Magritte will. So, for now, he makes sure no one bothers us when we go out around town. None of the street-kids, anyways. He can't do much about the soldiers. Or the mayor's sheriffs before that."

Clarick grinned suddenly. "I used to think he was a little sweet on Magritte. But then the pretty *unicorn-maiden* showed up..."

More or less out of necessity, Clarick knew that Thony wasn't a girl. He'd seen them up close enough while bringing their meals, after all.

Thony made a face and twisted his hair back into what he hoped was a *manly* short ponytail. A *queue,* was the proper term. He had to keep the hair longer than he liked for the unicorn-maiden gig. Puck and Amanita had insisted.

It hadn't occurred to him before that the children of a respectable innkeeper would be at risk of harassment. Now he remembered just how *many* raggedly dressed kids he had seen out in the streets. A group of them all together... and with Clarick so small...

"How old is Magritte?" he asked. "That's your sister, right?"

"Almost fifteen," Clarick answered. "Papa and Mama have insisted she and Mama stay in the back rooms since the soldiers arrived. We're not the only ones," he added with a certain world-weary tone. "It's like this every time an invading force goes through. The people old enough or young enough to be conscripted – or whatever – stay out of sight until the troops are gone."

"How often does this happen?" Thony asked with a certain horrified fascination. Puck had said something about this, but he hadn't been able to imagine it.

"At least every other year," Clarick said. "Papa says this time is a lot easier because I'm old enough to be more of a help. *Magritte* says that the parents want the older ones out of sight as much to keep them from deciding to join up and get out of Flowerdust as for any other reason. She's mortal tired of being stuck back there." He rolled his eyes. "It didn't help her case when she went on and on and *on* about how handsome Lieutenant Istevan is. But girls that age. What can you do?"

That sounded like a quote from his parents.

The almost-fifteen-year-old girls, Amanita and Dae, exchanged a dry look.

"Thanks, Clarick," Thony said before the girls decided to respond.

The boy nodded and headed back to his work.

"So… I guess I need to go see Jost," Amanita said, once the boy was out of earshot. "Dae, you need to stay out of sight, so you should go deliver Davril's stuff. You can take him the pack-donkey and bring Sandy back here."

"What if Davril needs to get away quickly?" Thony objected. "He can't ride that donkey."

"No," Dae agreed, somewhat unexpectedly to judge by Amanita's expression, "that shouldn't be an issue. Either he and Daphne are hidden well enough for now, or he won't have time to get out of there anyways."

Thony tilted his head slightly – it wasn't as if he could *hear* Twinklestar, but sometimes cocking his head made it easier to concentrate and pick up the unicorn's intention. "Twinklestar says you're right and that hollow is protected from casual detection. He says he also did... something... to reinforce those protections, too. So, they should be fine so long as they stay in there. And that they could *probably* even light a fire."

Dae looked impressed. "Cool. All right. I'll take him the donkey and his stuff. And bring back Sandy. That gives the three of *us* some mobility. 'Nita, are you going to take Thony with you when you go meet Jost?"

Thony folded his arms. That would likely involve things like putting on that stupid dress and pretending to be a girl. Amanita had suggested that keeping Jost from realizing that he'd been had might be a good thing. Thony disagreed, but he had to admit he could see it going that way as well. It kind of depended on how good a sense of humor this Jost-kid possessed.

"No," the runaway princess said. "I should probably go find out what he wants on my own. And maybe pick up some hair-dye in the market to tone down the color of Thony's hair so he doesn't stand out so much when he's 'out of uniform'."

That... sounded reasonable.

"I can keep a hood up," he offered, "but dyeing my hair *would* make it all easier."

And maybe keep this Jost-kid from catching on.

Amanita nodded. "You want to keep looking over all those letters and things? See if there's anything else that we need to know?"

He snorted lightly. "Yeah. As if."

But he gamely went back upstairs as the girls headed out on their errands.

An hour later, Thony stretched and then stood up. This was almost as bad as Master Eswith's protocol textbooks where he had expected Thony to decipher which of the nobles in the story was being snide to another one, which one was hiding something, and which one was just thoughtless. Thony had always wanted to refer to them as the traitor, the spy, and the booby-brain. Master Eswith had not been impressed.

The difference this time was that this was *real* and there probably *were* traitors and spies and booby-brains. He'd picked up on the estimable Captain Fayorn – the one who would be taking over Flowerdust from Shalladra – as a booby-brain.

There were a great many hints... but it was still frustrating that he didn't have Shalladra's half of the correspondence. And clearly the two of them – Shalladra and Raven'sWing – knew each other well enough that there was a great deal they didn't have to say explicitly. References to 'the flower' and 'the Grand Plan' were not particularly helpful.

There *was* a curious turn of phrase here and there, though. And the occasional line that had been crossed out or obliterated, with the former seeming to have been left readable intentionally for all that the lines through the words suggested that the reader *should* ignore what was written there.

It was almost as if Raven'sWing was trying to mislead *Shalladra* while still making her think she was privy to his every thought and plan.

But mislead his own top military woman for what purpose?

It was... annoying that Thony hadn't the slightest clue.

He was also getting – how had Clarick put it? – 'mortal tired' of sitting in this room. Although what applied to the boy's almost-fifteen-year-old sister as a reason to stay indoors probably applied to Thony as well. Likely *he* was old enough for the Raven troops to consider him conscriptable, even if Amanita and Dae's small stature made them less noticeable in that way.

But he simply could *not* stay here a moment longer.

Thony pulled on his coat and pulled the hood up. A cloak would be even better, but he'd noticed that no one here seemed to be wearing cloaks. And since the idea was to *not* stand out...

He tucked his purse inside his tunic and coat both – Amanita had passed on that bit of Jost's advice in a rather miffed tone, as if she should already have known that and felt dumb for having to be told. And then he went out.

The young prince had seen Flowerdust from above now – albeit at night – and was slightly less intimidated by the rabbit's warren of streets. But he had decided that if he didn't know his way about better, he'd be fairly useless in what he planned to do next.

Because Thony *planned* to do what *he* could to disrupt Valderon Raven'sWing's plans – whether that involved invading other worlds and threatening his own Aldyrwald, or just traveling around on this one and threatening Amanita's homeland. And Dae's, though he didn't really know where that was.

The tools he had were his own ingenuity and his skill in putting together pranks. Always before, he'd had to be careful to make sure there was no chance that anyone would get hurt. This time he could turn that on its head... even though he didn't really like the idea of causing harm.

The little streak of bad luck they'd begun in the Raven headquarters was a good start – and the girls had agreed that they would go back to work on it some more tonight. They would return those letters and the map at the same time.

But this *had* to be the last time they all worked together.

Amanita was absolutely right that it was too much of a risk for anyone to know who she was – and that made sending her out of the area the obvious solution. Especially now that she had Dae – and soon, Puck – to guard her and get her back to where she belonged.

Dae and Puck were likely to be on-board with this plan and Amanita... was most certainly *not* going to be.

Possibly he would have to get them to help tie her to Silverfoot's saddle – with a gag – and then to take her away.

Thony really wished *he* could go, too. This was a job for adults with military experience and armies and strong magick at their beck and call. Not a kid – or even a handful of kids – who knew how to prank people.

But you used what you had...

And to that end, Thony needed to understand the layout of Flowerdust's streets.

Which... was working out pretty well until he realized he was being followed.

And... surrounded.

By a pack of those raggedy street-kids.

In what wasn't really a back-street, but definitely wasn't one of the main thoroughfares.

There were three in front of him and Thony guessed, based on the way they were looking around that there were several more behind him.

Amanita had said that Jost had told her they'd be left alone...

...except Jost thought Thony was a *girl,* so even if these were *his* minions there was no safety for Thony here...

Darn.

"New t'town, are ye?" said a voice from behind him, and Thony turned, trying to at least put his back up against one of the walls so they couldn't come at him from all sides. The kids reminded him of the wolves the Royal Huntsman had described, surrounding a fawn in a pack; he didn't want to take his eyes off the ones in front of him.

"I am," he replied. "Who are you?"

A tall boy with a green cap strode in from the tightening circle of street-kids, taking center-stage. "Don' know 'at we need interductions an' all, now, lad. Yer coat an' boots'll do jest fine as a howdy-do."

Amanita had said Jost was a tall, skinny boy with a green cap. But wasn't she supposed to be meeting him? Were they done, and she'd gone back to the Starred Hoof?

Well, he didn't have a lot of options here...

Thony reached up and pulled off his hood. "If you're Jost, 'Nita said you're a friend to us."

No need to share her real identity with every street-kid in Flowerdust – and whomever they might sell it to.

The boy with the green cap stared at him.

One of the others – a short kid, with a kerchief knotted about his neck that might once have been red, and hair that was a dusty blonde – sniggered. "Di'n't y'say 'twas the 'corn-girl had fire-red hair, Jost? This'n don' look no *girl* t'me."

Jost reached out without looking and lightly cuffed the speaker on the head. "Aye, an' what would ye know of't, Skylir? Ain't decided what ye are yerself yet, aye?"

Skylir snorted, but stayed silent.

Jost narrowed his eyes at Thony.

"I *do* belong to the unicorn," Thony offered, trying to sound apologetic. He had a lot of practice at that, after all. "It was his idea, not mine. But then the adult we were traveling with made me put that white outfit on... said it should make us all safer if this really *was* a war-zone."

He sighed a little theatrically. "And then he *ditched* us and now..."

Thony shrugged.

"Hmmn." Jost looked around. "Well, there's not likely t'be two fireheads new in town this week. And I *did* tell those girls we'd be lookin' out for 'em. Fer all o' ye."

A boy with faded blue trousers kicked a pebble. "Dang, Jost. All this work an' nuttin' t'show fer it?"

Skylir gave a high, thin laugh. "Not like 'at's ne'er happened afore neither, Beel."

"Off wi' ye all," Jost said in a genial tone, but his gaze pinned Thony in place.

The rest scampered off, though there were a number of significant looks and off-color remarks that made Thony's face burn with embarrassment.

When they were entirely alone, Jost sized him up again. "Well. Quite a story."

Thony shrugged helplessly. "Sorry?"

The pack might be gone, but he still felt like prey.

"Hmmn." Jost stepped closer.

Thony forced himself not to shrink back into the stones of the wall behind him. It felt like he was being stalked. They were close to the same height, with Jost maybe a hair's-breadth taller. He looked half-starved, so Thony might outmass him... but doubtless *he* knew how to fight properly.

Or highly *im*properly but *effectively.*

And Thony... well, *didn't.* Even Roger and Jeremy's lessons back home had focused on the skills a prince was supposed to use – swordsmanship and archery – not commoner's skills like boxing and wrestling.

Or knife-fighting. The one thing that looked in pristine condition on Jost's body was the knife-hilt protruding from his worn leather boots.

"Ye sure ye're a boy?" Jost asked, raising a hand and running a finger along Thony's jawline. His finger was callused, the calluses ridged and sharp. It took another effort for Thony not to cringe away.

"I'm sure," he said dryly. "Why? Does the question come up a lot here?"

Jost chuckled at the rejoinder. "Well. Ye've got some spit in ye. Nay, not s'much as all 'at. Skylir there, a few others. Though more'n on t'streets than in housen, best I can tell."

Thony frowned at that. "Why's that?"

Jost raised an eyebrow. "Lots of parents don' tolerate such. Toss a kid out as wants t'ask the question, betimes."

"That's awful," Thony was shocked. "Their own *children?*"

"Lads 'n' lassies are s'posed t'follow their parents' direction," Jost said, watching the young prince closely. "Do as they say, work as they're bid, wed as they're told... *be* who they're told. And *what.*"

"What if they don't want to?" Thony asked, forgetting his own dire situation out of curiosity. The fact that *he* had to basically follow the line that Jost was describing was because he was born to royalty. Thony had watched his people live their lives with far more freedom.

146

Jost shrugged. "Why then, 'tis out on t'ear, most of 'em. A parent who shows more tolerance," he added, and there was a distant ring of sad knowledge in his voice, "soon finds theyselves t'object o' scorn an' derision by all 'round. Their business dries up, or their job is gi'en on. Money runs out an' t'whole fambly is like t'be out on t'streets an they stand 'gainst t'Way Things Are Meant To Be."

He enunciated the last few words carefully and in a fake stentorious tone, then cocked his head.

"Not t'way 'tis in yer land, la– lad? Thought ye must be from a farm out on t'plains."

Thony shook his head. "No, I'm from the mountains. And... no, it's not like that there." He winced. "Except for the royalty."

"Ah." Jost nodded wisely, as if he knew this sort of thing firsthand. "Need theyselves princes and princesses t'make more such, aye?"

That pretty much summed it up.

"Aye," Thony agreed, copying the other boy's mannerisms without noticing.

Jost smiled faintly. "Well-a-day. Sounds a right proper paradise then. Reckon ye'll be missing it there t'longer ye're gone."

Mama, Papa, Priscilla, Joanna, Roger, Jeremy, Wes, Tad... even Great-Uncle Sir Eddie and Master Eswith and Papa's obnoxious squires and Mama's fluttering ladies-in-waiting and the cooks and servants and village folk... Though definitely *not* the neighbors.

"Yes..." Thony swallowed a lump in his throat. "I... wanted to travel and see more than just home... but... now I can't go back any time soon..."

Jost looked sympathetic. "That 'corn o' yers, aye? Bad timing 'e 'ad t'get ye 'ere in the midst o' another invasion. Better t'have collected ye in a few months when it all blows o'er."

Thony frowned. "What do you mean?"

"Oh, we see these things all t'time," Jost almost sounded like he was boasting. "It ne'er lasts long. Raven troops this year, fellers from Isildor last, King Zielder's armies two before 'at. An' on an' on. We're in an unfortunate spot 'ere. Plen'y of lads an' lassies who wan' t' *travel an' see more'n home* go off wi' 'em an they pass through. An' plen'y of wounded or malingering soldiers manage to stay on."

The ragged boy shrugged. "'T'all works out in t'end."

What a... weird way to maintain population, Thony thought to himself.

Jost was looking at him thoughtfully again, though. "Not a lass. But near as pretty as 'un. An' Bound to the 'corn, ye say?"

Thony nodded warily.

A careful look to each side, and Jost stepped... uncomfortably close. He lowered his voice to a whisper. "I've a yen t'... *travel an' see more'n home* meself. Gettin' old fer the streets, aye? An' no shot at an honorable line o' work after."

Thony really couldn't back up... maybe putting his back against the wall hadn't been such a great idea after all.

"Um... and what do you want me to do about it?" He kept his own voice quiet, again responding to the other boy's manner.

Jost leaned in and whispered directly into Thony's ear. "When ye leave – ye take me with. An'... in return, I'll aid ye here as I can."

Thony blinked. It felt... very weird to have someone's words tickling his ear. "That's... more than you asked of, um, 'Nita."

Jost snorted lightly, and that was even weirder. "I asked 'er t' see I got a word wit' ye. Any'un can see she's but a wee lass... for all that she knows towns better'n ye. Figured ye were t'one callin' t'shots."

"Oh." Thony blinked. "Um... sure?"

He *wasn't* sure, not at *all*. But he had no idea how to get out of this situation without saying 'yes.' And after all, he wasn't likely to be leaving Flowerdust anytime soon.

Puck had said he'd be gone between a week and two weeks – and this was only three days.

And even when he got back, Puck and Amanita – and likely Dae – would leave, but Thony... *couldn't*.

Hmmmn. Maybe he *could* use this offer of *help*...

"Um..." he added, still softly, since Jost's ear was right by his own mouth. He tried not to breathe into it. "The girls have to go on, but I'm... *I'm* not leaving for awhile. The sorcerer-dude who these Raven troops look to – he's coming here. And we've figured out that his plans threaten my... my homeland. I'm going to try to stop him."

Jost straightened up a little at that to look into Thony's eyes in surprise. His own were a light green. "All on yer lonesome?"

Thony looked down and away. It sounded stupid when stated out loud.

But... "Alone if I must." He looked up at Jost out of the corner of his eye. "With your help, if you're still offering."

The other boy drew in a breath and gave him a look that Thony couldn't really interpret – well, except for the incredulous part. He was used to people giving him incredulous looks, after all.

"Well-a-day." Jost rocked back on his heels a little. "I s'pose I *did* offer."

Thony breathed a sigh of relief – he had a little bit of his personal space back *and* he had an ally. That gave him much better odds of surviving his crazy plans... and stopping a sorcerous invasion of Aldyrwald wasn't really helpful if the result was only to expose his country to dismemberment by its neighbors if he didn't make it home with a princess in tow and a father-in-law with knights and armies to lend him.

"Thank you," he said, letting some of that heartfelt relief into his tone.

Jost blinked a couple of times, then shook his head, again with that odd expression.

"Not a lass, 'e says." Jost shook his head once more. "I'm thinkin' mayhap it doesn' matter."

Thony frowned. "What are you talking about?"

The other boy chuckled. "Ye're not as old as ye look, fer all yer height, I think. An' a 'corn-girl atop 't'all. Well, we'll see.

"Can ye howl like a wolf? Or hoot like an owl?"

"I... think so," Thony said, confused by the change of topic.

Well, and confused by the first topic as well.

Jost gave him a one-sided smile. "That's how ye call an ye hae need then, aye? A wolf an 'tis a pack ye need. An owl an 'tis jus' me, meself ye want. T'come an' find ye," he added a little hurriedly.

Thony gave him a cautious smile back. "Okay. And 'Nita said she promised we'd help you guys out if need be. How do I know when you want me to come find *you?*"

The leader of the street-kids laughed. "Don' worry yer pretty wee head on that. I'll see ye're sent word."

That was... both reassuring and offensive.

But Thony wasn't exactly in a position to complain.

"All right."

Jost stepped back again and tipped his hat to Thony. "Keep that hood down, aye? So's we know who ye are."

Thony nodded. "All right."

Jost nodded and turned, striding away firmly.

Thony slumped against the wall. This 'adventure' just kept raising the bar on what he considered his 'most terrifying experience ever.' Home was sounding better and better...

But if he'd stayed home, he'd be looking at a marriage to an elderly middleborn princess with orders to kill him and Papa both at her earliest convenience.

And if he'd stayed home, he'd never have learned about this potential sorcerous and military attack coming.

Sometimes... you just had to accept that things were going to get weird.

But doubtless Amanita was going to have several sharp things to say to him about this latest episode. And since she was likely to hear about it from Jost or someone even if Thony didn't tell her – and since he now had a reason *not* to dye his hair, since it was being used to identify him on the streets – he probably needed to man up and just tell her himself.

Resolutely, Thony started back to the Inn of the Starred Hoof.

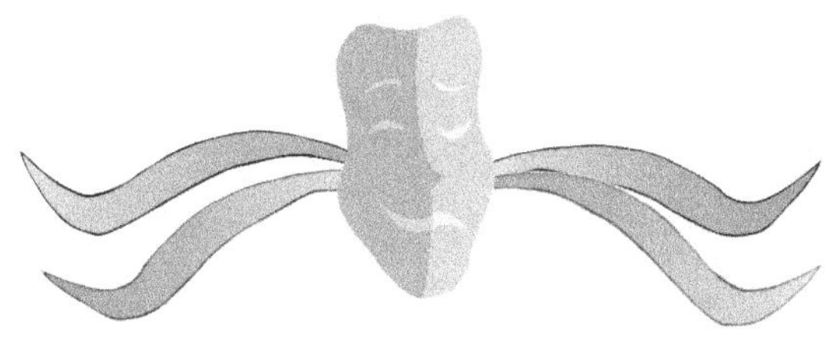

Chapter TWELVE

Unmistaken Identities

UNFORTUNATELY, HE'D GOTTEN TURNED AROUND somewhere and his harrowing experience with Jost had somewhat scrambled his memories. When Thony found himself on the outskirts of town, he had to admit he'd gotten lost.

On the other hand, he *now* knew where he was. It was a simple matter to get from here to the town center, and from there to the Inn of the Starred Hoof. Conveniently, it was past lunchtime and that path would take him past most of the foodstalls.

He started to head back when he realized that something had caught his eye when he looked out on the eastern road. A puff of dust...

Someone coming in from the direction that Valderon Raven's Wing was located...

Even as he watched, the puff of dust far down the road began to look more like a small group of riders, approaching quickly. In moments it was possible to tell that the tiny figures wore the same bright blue as the Raven troops in Flowerdust.

Thony decided to stay where he was and see what he could figure out.

The riders brought their lathered horses down to a walk several hundred feet short of his position, but rather deeper into the edges of the town than the young prince would have thought wise. Chickens and geese scattered from in front of them with loud squawks, half-running, half-flying back into their yards as the horses slowed.

Several of the riders chuckled at the sight.

One of them started out to lead the rest, then was gently nudged to a secondary position by another rider. The others formed up more carefully behind the two leaders.

"You haven't been here before any more than I have," the second rider was saying in a gently amused tone to the one who had taken the first position as they approached where Thony was artistically leaning against a building, trying to look like he belonged.

"You shouldn't be out front in an unpacified location, milord," said the first fellow – whose drooping mustaches and long pale-blonde hair didn't conceal his youth. He couldn't have been much over twenty.

"From all the reports it *is* a pacified location, Fayorn," the second rider replied. He looked to be quite a bit older – or so the wings of white starting at his temples and contrasting sharply with his black hair suggested. "The bigger problem is just finding our way around. It's supposed to be fairly labyrinthine."

"To slow down invaders, doubtless," someone else noted.

"So they can sell them things," said a fourth.

There was a laugh all around at that sally... It wasn't as cynical a laugh as Thony would have expected.

The older man laughed along with the rest, then added, "Shalladra said there weren't any maps when she arrived and she's had a devil of a time finding anyone qualified to do the work."

"Hunh." The blonde man in front seemed skeptical.

"You, boy," the man with the black-and-white hair called out to Thony, reining in close beside the runaway prince, "do you know your way to the mayoral mansion?"

Since that had been where he was headed – and since his own estimation of Flowerdust agreed with theirs – Thony nodded warily.

The man with the two-toned hair smiled down at him kindly. "What hair you have, lad! I could wish for a son as well-built as you. And with such hair! Can you point us in the right direction?"

Thony resisted the urge to pull his hood back up. "Um, it's kind of complicated... sir."

The man chuckled. "So, I've heard. Here, then. Climb up here behind me and show us the way, will you? I'll give you a penny for your trouble," he added when Thony hesitated still.

If he really were the poor kid he was portraying, that would be an irresistible temptation, Thony guessed.

Trying not to show his reluctance, he reached up to take the man's offered hand. The man took his foot out of the stirrup so Thony could use it for his own climb onto the tall, black horse caparisoned in that vivid blue. The rider, he noted, was dressed all in black with touches of silver... unlike his men.

The blonde soldier ahead looked vaguely disapproving, as did at least one of the men behind, but neither one spoke, and Thony avoided their eyes as he settled himself astride the horse and behind the man.

"That way, sir," he said, taking a hand off the man's waist to point in the correct direction.

"See, Fayorn," the rider in black said. "We'd likely have run into trouble immediately without our young friend here."

The blonde man – Captain Fayorn – grunted and led off.

And Thony rode back in to Flowerdust on the back of Valderon Raven'sWing's saddle.

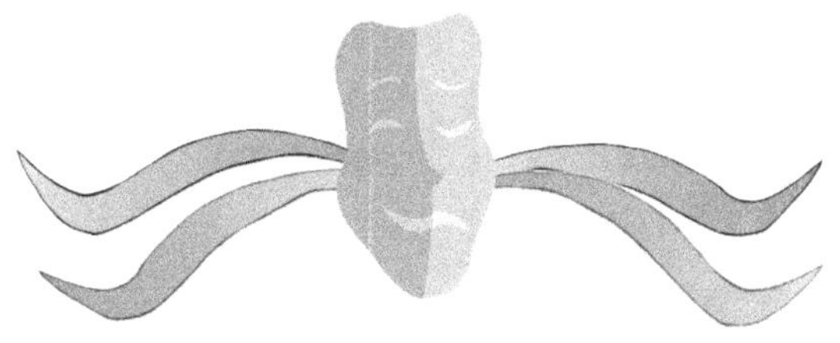

EPILOGUE

"**I** STILL THINK WE SHOULD check in at the Guildhouse," the man said very quietly. "She'll likely have been there already herself."

They were seated at a table in a quiet corner of the commonroom of a well-appointed inn.

His companion shook her head. "You heard what they were saying in the square. Anyone that looks like a mercenary is being conscripted immediately. They even took *Tethro Fishglitter*, and he's been too lame to fight for five years. Checking in at the Guildhouse would mark us, even if we don't *look* like mercenaries right now."

"Well, I suppose it's a good thing no would believe Dae is a mercenary by *looking* at her then," Daennor Cat'sfoot said dryly. "No matter how many large weapons she insists on toting around everywhere."

Kamauri Spiralspear gave him a reproving look. "You're still annoyed because she outshot you when we had her in hand last? Or because she was able to sneak past *you?*"

The man snorted. "And *you* and *Rainsparkle.* The girl is gifted at sneaking, I'll say that. But her commonsense could use a little work."

"Fair enough." Kamauri sighed. She leaned on his shoulder. "Thank goodness we decided to try sneaking up on *her* this time and left everything that might identify us visually out with the equines."

Daennor slipped an arm around her waist. "Yes. I wouldn't have guessed how bad it is here just to look at it. At least the inns are cheap with all the patronage chased away," he added dryly.

She relaxed into his hold for a moment, then pulled away. "Cheap enough to rent separate rooms," she said, standing up. "I'll speak to the innkeeper about accommodations."

"Kamauri..." He caught at her hand.

The woman gave him a sad, but determined look back. "It's who I am, Daennor. Nothing has really changed." She tapped a necklace that dangled down over her fawn-colored leather tunic. It was a central slice of one of the long cone-shaped turritella shells, but resembled what the cross-section of a unicorn-horn might look like. If anyone was venal and cruel – and *stupid* – enough to have a horn without its owner. "Spiralspear. Without Rainsparkle... I don't even really have an *identity.*"

"You'd have *me,*" Daennor said softly. "We could... stop all this nonsense. Buy a farm. Adopt Dae. Let her grow up properly... Have a few of our own..."

Kamauri gave him a sad smile. "Oh, lo– my friend. We've been over this before. We both worked too hard for these skills. And neither one of us has the money – yet – to live that dream."

"We might *together*," he argued, with the tone of someone doing it for the umpteenth time. But he had to add "A *small* farm anyways," out of honesty.

"We don't know anything about growing things," Kamauri pointed out.

"We can learn," he retorted. "Being a unicorn-maiden isn't supposed to last your whole *life,* Kamauri."

Gently, she freed her fingers.

"We'll talk about it when we've gotten Dae out of here and settled her someplace safe."

She walked away towards the bar.

"So, you said the *last* time we caught up with that accident-prone hellion," Daennor sighed with resignation and a certain amount of frustrated resentment. "And the time before *that.*

"Will there *ever* be a 'right time,' Kamauri?"

Map from Captain Shalladra's Bedroom

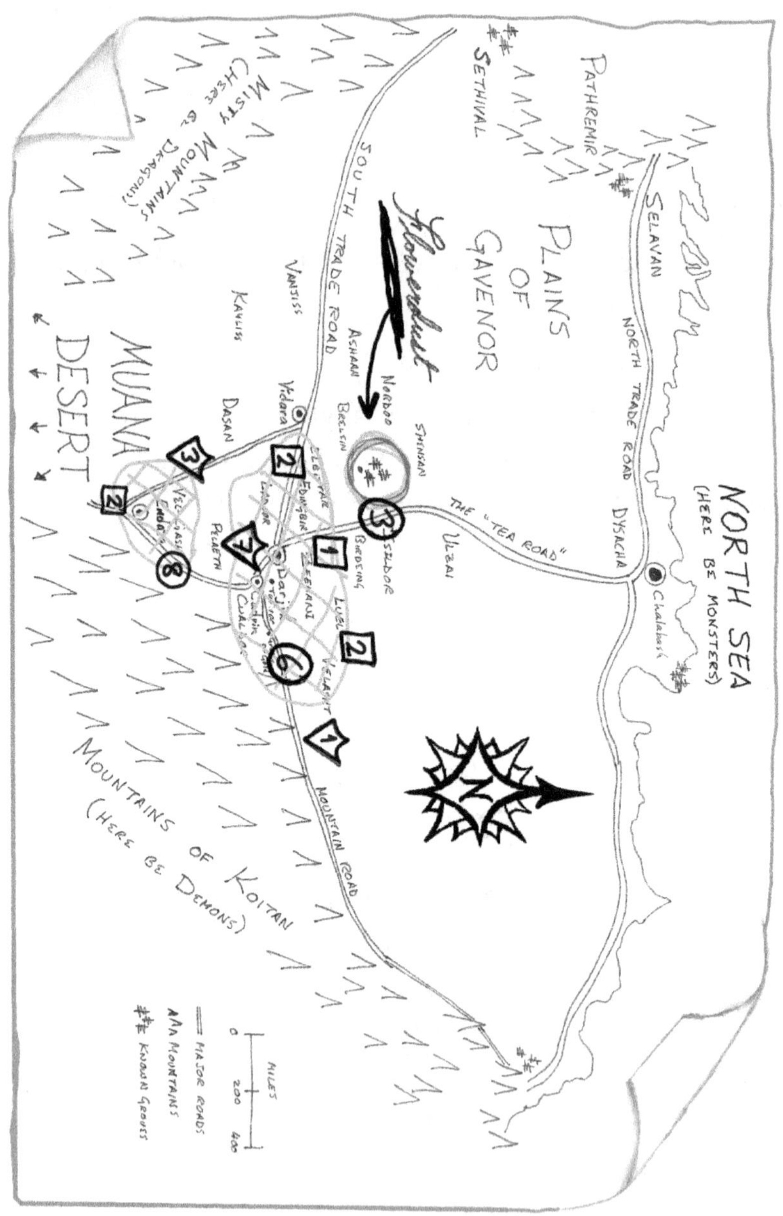

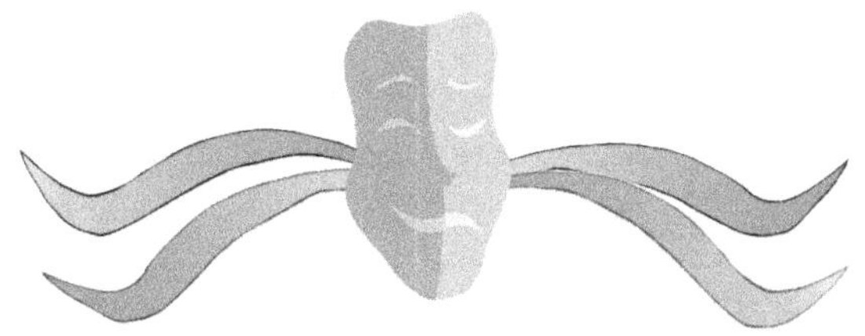

Index of Characters

- **Important People in Flowerdust now:**

• **Amanita (a.k.a. 'Nita).** A foreign girl who used to work in the Aldyrwald castle kitchens, and most recently worked in the stables. She came from another world beyond the Fairy Wood.

• **Beel.** A street-kid in Jost's gang in Flowerdust.

• **Clarick.** The nine-year-old son of the innkeeper of the Inn of the Starred Hoof in Flowerdust.

• **Dae Goldeneyes.** Youngest mercenary ever. A graduate of Sonoro's School of Soldiering.

• **Daennor Cat'sFoot.** Mercenary. Partner of Kamauri Spiralspear. A graduate of Sonoro's School of Soldiering.

• **Daphne.** An associate of Julanna Silversea.

• **Davril (a.k.a., Dav).** An associate of Julanna Silversea.

• **Evrien Quickfoot.** A very old mercenary. Temporary Guildhouse-Keeper in Flowerdust. A graduate of Arazia's Academy at Arms.

• **Fayorn.** A captain in Valderon Raven'sWing's army.

• **Istevan Highblade (called Slyblade, a.k.a Stev).** A mercenary serving as a lieutenant in the Raven-troops in Flowerdust. Also a spy helping Julanna Silversea. A graduate of Sonoro's School of Soldiering.

• **Jost.** Leader of a gang of street-kids in Flowerdust.

• **Julanna Silversea.** A Bard spying on Valderon Raven'sWing's forces in Flowerdust. She has a nursing baby.

161

• **Kamauri Spiralspear.** Mercenary and unicorn-maiden. Bound to Rainsparkle, partner with Daennor Cat'sFoot. Friend of Dae Goldeneyes. A graduate of Sonoro's School of Soldiering.

• **Louris.** Street-kid.

• **Magritte.** The fifteen-year-old daughter of the innkeeper of the Inn of the Starred Hoof. Clarick's sister.

• **Rainsparkle.** Unicorn. Bound to Kamauri Spiralspear.

• **Shalladra Stillheart (called 'Icicleblood').** Valderon Raven'sWing's Captain-Mayoress in Flowerdust.

• **Silverfoot.** Thony's rather-too-energetic horse.

• **Skylir.** A street-kid in Jost's gang.

• **Thony (Prince Anthony Devinthal the Affable and the Affirmative).** Crown Prince of Aldyrwald. Younger brother of Princess Joanna and Princess Priscilla. Unicorn-maiden Bound to Twinklestar.

• **Twinklestar.** Unicorn, Bound to Thony, friend of Amanita.

• **Valderon Raven'sWing.** An Evil Wizard.

Back on Thony's homeworld:

• **Annabel (Queen Annabel of Aldyrwald).** Wife of King Bill; mother of Joanna, Priscilla, and Thony. Youngest of seven sisters and three brothers.

• **Bill (King Bill / King William Devinthal of Aldyrwald).** Husband of Queen Annabel. Father of Joanna, Priscilla, and Thony. Oldest of seven brothers.

• **Cythera.** Seeress and Goddess of Fire on the world where Aldyrwald is located.

• **Eddie (Great-Uncle Sir Eddie / Prince Edward of Aldyrwald).** A middle-born brother of King Bill's father, Grandpa Tom. Thony's riding master.

• **Eswith (Master Eswith).** Protocol master of the Aldyrwald royal family.

• **Jeremy.** Centaur male. Husband of Priscilla. Son of Caspar and Mariah.

• **Janet (Queen Janet of Schwannsberg).** Wife of King Richie. Mother of Prince Raymond, Prince Sir Roger, Prince Ryan, Princess Laura, Princess Sophia, and Princess Tessa.

• **Joanna (Princess Joanna Devinthal the Wise and Wonderful).** Eldest-born princess of Aldyrwald. Daughter of King Bill and Queen Annabel; sister of Priscilla and Thony. Wife of Prince Sir Roger. Goddess of the Earth.

• **Paul.** Journeyman pastry chef in the Aldyrwald royal kitchens. (Amanita calls him 'Mr. Grabby-Hands')

• **Phillip.** Sorcerer and God of Water on the world where Aldyrwald is located. Husband of Cythera.

• **Priscilla (Princess Priscilla Devinthal the Bright-Eyed and Bushy-Tailed, aka Prissy).** Second-born princess of Aldyrwald. Daughter of King Bill and Queen Annabel; sister of Joanna and Thony. Wife of Jeremy. Goddess of Animals (including humans) and of Love/Fertility.

• **Richie (King Richie of Schwannsberg).** Husband of Queen Janet. Father of Prince Raymond, Prince Sir Roger, Prince Ryan, Princess Laura, Princess Sophia, and Princess Tessa.

• **Roger (Prince of Schwannsberg and Knight).** Second-born son of King Richie and Queen Janet; younger brother of Prince Raymond and Princess Laura; older brother of Prince Ryan, Princess Sophia, and Princess Tessa. Husband of Joanna. God of Air.

• **Tad/Thaddeus.** Stablemaster to Aldyrwald Castle, Amanita's boss.

• **Wesley (Wes).** Stableboy in the Aldyrwald royal stables.

• **People Who are Elsewhere, but Still Important:**

• **Aspenheart, Lord.** Prince of the Light-elves, an attendant of the Fairy Queen.

• **Chhilabiaen.** Fairy-mare. Steed of Puck.

• **Ederard.** King of Canador, Prince Harper's father.

• **Elivia.** Princess-Consort-to-be of Canador. Prince Harper's betrothed.

• **Girona Starshine.** A student wizard from Happy-Go-Lucky on Eyola, cousin to Midele.

• **Harper.** Crown Prince of Canador. Dae Goldeneyes used to be his bodyguard.

• **Lascha Lohrstorser.** The Duchess of Middleveld in Canador.

• **Lilysong.** The Fairy Queen… also the Great Goddess Who Guards the Ways Between the Worlds.

• **Midele Featherspray.** A novice priestess of the Golden Sphinx on Eyola, Girona's cousin.

• **Mithral.** King of Selevan.

• **Opalsinger, Lady.** Princess of the Dark-elves, attendant of the Fairy Queen.

• **Puck.** The 'King of Pranksters', a fairy attendant of Queen Lilysong.

• **Quellarie.** Someone who advised Amanita on how to travel the Fairy Wood.

• **Raellia.** Queen of Widdenward. She hired Dae to guard a loomhouse.

• **Tameran.** King of Sethival.

• **Taridanae Foxheart (a.k.a. the Fox).** Headmistress of Sonoro's School of Soldiering. Granddaughter of Sonoro.

• **Tethro Fishglitter.** Former Mercenary Guildhouse-Keeper in Flowerdust. A conscript into the Raven-troops.

• **Zielder.** A king who invaded through Flowerdust a couple of years ago.

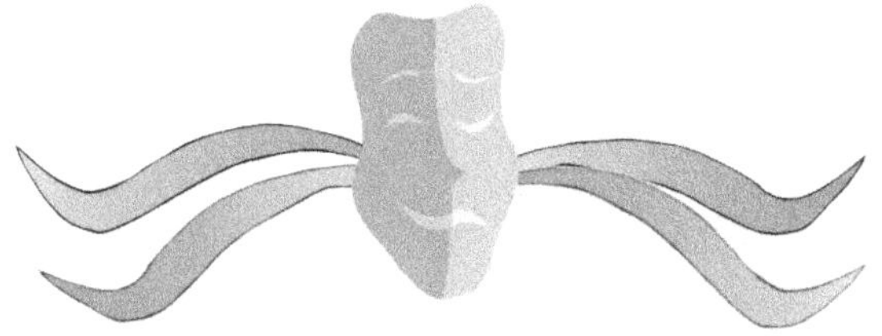

Index of Places

- **On Thony's homeworld:**

  • **Aldyrwald.** The country where Thony is Crown Prince. Three linked valleys, centrally located in the mountain region.

  • **Schwannsberg.** A two-valley kingdom immediately adjacent to Aldyrwald, Roger's homeland. Ruled by King Richie and Queen Janet.

- **Other worlds:**

  • **Eyola.** The world that Midele and Girona are from.

  • **Fairy Wood.** Ruled by Queen Lilysong. A forest that bridges the gap between many worlds. Only the fairies and elves know how to navigate it by nature, though others can learn.

  • **Happy-Go-Lucky.** Girona's homeland on Eyola.

  • **Perushin village.** Accessed via the Fairy Wood and inhabited by the Perushin – a species of unusual magickal beings.

- **Amanita's homeworld:**

  • **Arazia's Academy at Arms.** A school for mercenaries. A former graduate is Evrien Quickfoot.

  • **Brelsin.** A country in the plains that regularly gets overrun by invaders. On Amanita's homeworld. East of Pathremir, Sethival, Selavan, Plains of Gavenor, Dawil, the Merutian Sea.

  • **Cadrin.** A town lying few weeks east of Flowerdust.

  • **Canador.** A country ruled by King Ederard.

• **Darjil.** A town about ten days' ride from Flowerdust.

• **Dawil.** A prosperous country very far to the west of Flowerdust.

• **Flowerdust.** A small nowhere-sort of town in Brelsin.

• **Grains-of-Gold.** A town lying a few weeks east of Flowerdust.

• **Indistran.** A city not terribly far from Flowerdust.

• **Inn of the Starred Hoof.** An inn in Flowerdust where only the desperate and down-on-their-luck ever stay.

• **Isildor.** A country that invaded through Flowerdust a year ago.

• **Merutian Sea.** An ocean very far to the west of Flowerdust.

• **Middleveld.** A duchy in the country of Canador.

• **Misty Mountains.** The mountain-range where Pathremir is located.

• **Mountains of Koitan.** Where Arazia's Academy at Arms is located

• **Pathremir.** A country in the Misty Mountains. Amanita's homeland

• **Plains of Gavenor.** An area west of Brelsin.

• **Selavan.** A country ruled by King Mithral. West of Brelsin, adjacent to Pathremir and the Plains of Gavenor. Includes a famous school for Bards and an enclave for unicorn-maidens.

• **Sethival.** A country ruled by King Tameran. West of Brelsin and adjacent to Pathremir.

• **Sonoro's School of Soldiering.** Famous school for mercenaries. Graduates include the current headmistress, Taridanae Foxheart, Istevan Highblade, Kamauri Spiralspear, Daennor Cat'sFoot, and Dae Goldeneyes.

• **Tarivor.** A town lying a few weeks east of Flowerdust.

• **Widdenward.** A country ruled by Queen Raellia.

Author's Note

WOW! The **THIRD BOOK** of the *Prankster Prince!*

If this were a trilogy, I'd be done!

Of course, this isn't a trilogy, because Thony and Amanita (and Dae [and Twinklestar]) still have to save all the worlds beyond the Fairy Wood… and possibly Amanita and Dae's world as well. And defeat an Evil Wizard. And get Amanita back home. And find Thony a princess-bride…

Okay, we've got four-ish more books to go.

It's still a big milestone for me, though. This is the third book in any of the main lines of my series *(mostly because I decided to mix things up with the **Knightess of the Realm** series)*. I'll hit Book Number Three in each of those series by the end of Summer 2024… and that's with adding in a **Knightess of the Realm prequel novella** about how Kefen and Ivan met as pages *(ssshhhh! Don't tell anyone I told you!)*.

And that clearly means that it's time to start a NEW series going along. The new series, *Tales of the Turquoise Empire,* will debut this year. As the name implies, there are a LOT of stories to be told in the World of the Living Gods.

Which I should explain a bit about.

I've been calling Karana and Amanita's (and Dae's) world 'the World of the Living Gods' in my head for Ages. It feels like there's a better name out there… but I haven't been able to figure it out yet. Naturally, it's not what anyone there actually calls the place, but with Gods and Goddesses wandering all over it, it's the one that has made sense to me. To paraphrase something the person who inspired Amanita once told me (about something else entirely), you can't throw a rock on this planet without hitting a God.

(Not that I recommend trying that. Even if several of the Gods our Brave Adventurers are running into take a rather humorous view of such things. It's just not a good arena to mess around in, given that you don't know if the next one will or not.)

And, as I mentioned in the Author's Note for ***An Entirely-Unexpected Revelation: Book Two of the Heir's Journey (A Knightess of the Realm Novel)*** *(phew!)* I'm separating out my *noms de plume:*

From here on out, FICTION will be under the name Mangala McNamara, and NON-fiction will be under the name Kerridwen McNamara. Hopefully that will make it easier for you to find what you are looking for (and not the other stuff) and I hope you'll bear with me through the ugly middle of this while I am re-organizing things. If you can't find a particular book when you are looking for it (because the sorting algorithms are confused), just email me (<u>RisingDragonBooks@gmail.com</u>) or check my website (<u>https://www.RisingDragonBooks.com</u>).

About the Author

Mangala McNamara lives in Flyover Country (the far northern end of the US South) with her husband, The Professor, and four of her six children. The remaining children are in college – you can blame the oldest for the excessive amounts of math showing up in Mangala's fantasy novels, the second one for better attention to staging of scenes, the third for all the economics, and the fourth for great attention to history – and all of them for a focus on political science! Mangala is a former professional bellydance instructor, and used to enjoy knitting, crotchet and embroidering Temari balls but now is much more boring as she rarely does anything but write... although she also fences (the sport) and plays D&D with her kids. She owes her love of books and reading to her mother, who was a professional folklorist and could recite – from memory – stories from every nation in the United Nations.

Her **Knightess of the Realm** and **Chronicles of Ilseador** series occur in Amanita's homeworld.

Also by Mangala McNamara

Fantasy in the World of the Living Gods:

The Prankster Prince

Thony and the Much-Anticipated Adventure: Book One of The Prankster Prince

Thony Goes Astray! (in the Deep, Dark, and Dangerous Fairy Wood): Book Two of The Prankster Prince

So You Want to Be a Hero? Book Three of the Prankster Prince

Knightess of the Realm

A Not-So-Sacrificial Maiden

Out of the Woods… Hopefully (a Prequel Novella)

A Not-So-Simple Mission: Book One of the Heir's Journey

An Entirely-Unexpected Revelation: Book Two of the Heir's Journey

The Chronicles of Ilseador

The Rebel Duchess: Book One

The King's Champion: Book Two

More Fantasy coming soon…

An All-Too-Surprising Homecoming: Book 3 of the Heir's Journey (A Knightess of the Realm Novel)

The Pirate-King: Book Three of the Chronicles of Ilseador (April 2024)